The most gentle of hearts

Anne Olga Vea

ISBN: 978-82-93355-59-5

The sunset was throwing a golden glow over everything and the wind had died down. The huge stable complex was normally teeming with life but at the moment it was rather quiet there. Just the people and the horses they were tending too were moving about. The huge area was hosting the final competitions this year and the entire equestrian community were there in person or at least following every event with sharp eyes through the media. The very best riders and horses from all over the world were gathered there and there were several competitions each day. The very high ranking riders were among the world elite and so were their horses, these were athletes on an Olympic level and the press was making bets about who would be the ones winning the final competitions within the different disciplines.

The stable known as North B was among the largest there, it could house about a hundred and fifty horses and this was where the eventing horses and the show jumpers and dressage horses were placed during the five day long competition. Not all the boxes were occupied though, some were filled with equipment due to a shortage of storage space. By one of those equipment storages a woman was busy preparing a saddle, she was sitting on a bench while going over the leather making it shine and she had tied her long mahogany hair back into a tight bun. She wore riding pants and a west and she was humming as she was working. She was lucky enough to have gotten storage right next to the box where her horse were to live and now she was listening to him chewing his hay happily. She was a three day eventer and the two first competitions were already done, now the dressage part was left and it would determine who the winner was this year. She had faced some very stiff competition this year, but she was most definitely among the favourites. Mostly thanks to the huge bay gelding who stuck his head out of the box, sending her curious glances. Adagio was a very rare horse, huge and seemingly clumsy but he could jump and run like none other and he could even be elegant when asked to. She would have a good chance the next day.

She had bought the gelding four years earlier and they had become a good team over the years, he was fourteen now, at his peak and among the best eventing horses in the world. Some said that he was too tall and too lanky to really perform well but she had proven them otherwise. Her Adagio was perhaps a mix breed of dubious parentage but that didn't matter, he had talent and the courage of a lion mixed with a willingness which was rare to find in a horse. She did regard herself as lucky to have found him and he was like a family member to her. She finished working on the tack and her stable hand came sauntering by, Linda was a small lean girl of 19, her big dream was to become an eventer too and she had talent but she wasn't yet experienced enough to ride the high classes and she did have some trouble with a leg she had broken as a kid. It made it hard for her to keep her balance perfectly over the jumps and she had taken some nasty tumbles over the years.

Isadora got up and shook out the saddle blanket she had been sitting on, Linda stopped and took a peek into Adagio's box. "He is as calm as a cucumber"

Isadora nodded. "He is, he has food, that makes him happy, competition or no competition"

Linda petted the huge bay on the neck and checked that the horse hadn't pooped in the sawdust since she cleaned the box earlier that evening. "So, what do you think about tomorrow?"

Isadora was about to answer when they both became aware of a man running past them like his pants were on fire. He was holding a cell phone and he was a bit pale. Linda frowned. "Wasn't that…"

Isadora nodded. "Mr Brewster, could something be wrong?"

The stable was built in an L shape and Mr Brewster was one of the eventers, people said that he was ranking as number three below Isadora and another rider who also had his horse in this stable. The horse Mr Brewster rode wasn't owned by him, it was a horse owned by a huge business cooperation and he sort of rented the animal and was sponsored by the cooperation. Isadora closed the box door and walked up the stable floor, the majority of the horses were stabled in the top wing of the building and that was where Mr Brewster's mare Crested Moon was kept. Linda and Isadora stopped, there were several people in front of the box where the mare was kept, some were arguing and they saw that the groom, a woman by the name of Anna was standing there, looking as if she was in despair. Linda wetted her lips. "Those two over there, they are the official vets working here"

Isadora felt a sting of worry, with that many horses gathered in one place over almost a week there were bound to be some problems and horses do get sick. She just didn't want Mr Brewster to lose the competition just because of something happening to Moon. They were competitors but most of the riders knew each other very well and were if not friends at least very respectful towards each other. You had to be, the eventers were a sort of clan within the equestrian community, the sport was so dangerous they lost people and horses almost every year and it gave them a special sort of connection.

Isadora saw that her other main rival was there, standing outside of the box of his horse and she gathered her composure and walked over. She knew of no other man who rode as well as him, and he was both famous and a bit of an enigma. People knew close to nothing about him and almost every woman and some men too within the community had a major crush on him. Isadora most certainly did but he never seemed to care about anything except his horse and the sport. She could just admire him from a distance and dream, dreams she knew were never coming true.

He was staring at the commotion outside of Moon's box with a worried frown and she knew that nobody there wanted to win just because someone else's horse got sick or injured. They all loved horses, and they loved the sport too.

She nodded politely at him. “Mr Oswold, do you know what is wrong?”

The very tall blonde man sent her a swift smile. “Good evening Ms Singer, I think Moon is having a bout of stomach trouble. Brent just ran off to call for the animal ambulance, the vets wants to take her to the animal hospital”

They heard a horse whinnying in obvious distress from the mare’s box and a massive silvery grey stallion peeked out from the box behind Mr Oswold. Silver Ghost was regarded as the best eventing horse ever, his courage and will to win was famous and so was his rider. Those two together made everything seem possible and she knew that Mr Oswold had raised the stallion himself. “Oh no, I hope it isn’t anything serious?”

The blonde looked a bit sad. “So do I, Brent has been looking forward to beating me, and I fear that Mr Berner will want to skin him alive if something happens to that mare”

Isadora had to grin, Mr Berner was the CEO of the cooperation which owned Crested Moon and he was a former horse trainer and he ran his business the same way as he had run his training stables, with iron will and iron discipline. But he adored horses and Isadora had met him a few times and liked the brusque old man, he was a hard nut but very honest and fair.

They heard sirens and a huge vehicle entered the wide stable doors at the top of the building, Mr Brewster was running next to it, gesticulating. They watched as Anna lead the gorgeous cream coloured mare into the ambulance, the horse was sweating profusely and the large lovely eyes wide with pain. She tried to kick her own stomach several times and one of the vets entered the ambulance to administer some tranquilizer. Brent stood there, looking like a man in despair and Anna petted his back, as if to comfort him. The grooms and the riders were a part of a team and had to know and trust each other, and they had to cooperate all the time to make sure that the horses were ready and capable of doing their very best. Mr Oswold walked over and Brent sent him a pale grin, Anna looked worried too. Linda pulled at Isadora's sleeve. "I will go and make sure Adagio has enough hay and a night blanket and some fresh water, then I will call it a night. Tomorrow at five thirty?"

Isadora nodded. "Five thirty it is, do not forget to add some salt to his gruel, he will need it"

She didn't have to tell Linda what to do, the girl already knew but Isadora was in fact a bit nervous. It was her first chance at the title of champion and she didn't want to lose it simply because Adagio felt sluggish. The huge gelding was not an ideal dressage horse but he could be technically perfect, she just had to make sure that he didn't do any mistakes. The fact that he wasn't as pretty to look at as Crescent Moon or Silver Ghost wasn't his fault. There were others too in the competition, fifteen more riders but they weren't regarded as potential winners. None of them had scored that high on the first two parts of the competition and Isadora knew that at least one of them was contemplating withdrawing from the last part of the three day competition. Anna and Mr Brewster did leave, they were probably driving to get to the animal hospital to be with Moon and Mr Oswold shook his head. "Too bad, that mare didn't look well at all. Could it be something serious?"

Isadora saw that many others had gathered there too, worried and disturbed by the sudden and unforeseen sickness. "She was really in a lot of pain, could be a twisted gut?"

Mr Oswold frowned. "Then he won't be able to compete for months, not on that mare at least. She'll need surgery and a long time to recover too"

Isadora sighed. "Let us hope it is just something minor, he doesn't deserve this. He has fought so hard to reach this level"

Mr Oswold smiled rather fondly. "Yes, he has, I am lucky to be able to call him a friend, and I will keep my fingers crossed"

He tilted his head. "If you are done for the day we could go for a beer? The beer tent is not far away and they do actually have decent beer, not just the swill other places do serve at such festivals."

Isadora did blush slightly, Mr Oswold was the favourite of the crowds, the huge man on the giant silvery steed was making girls swoon and she had to admit that he was almost terrifyingly handsome. Some said he was an arrogant asshole but she had seen that he was far from it, it was just a façade to keep the media at bay, the sport didn't get that much of a crowd but they did attract some attention and it was just as important to them as to other athletes to stay focused and in control. She had met him many times and he usually kept everybody at an arm's length. He didn't even have a groom but took care of everything himself and he was polite and well behaved but also very private.

Some said that his family in fact was royalty from some old European country which didn't exist anymore and Isadora could believe it, he looked majestic and she had never encountered anyone that good with horses, he seemed to be able to talk to them. And he was also a very firm protector of animals, she had once seen him beat the crap out of a guy who tried to ride his horse in a competition using a spade bit and another time he had bought a horse the owner wanted to send off to slaughter just because it was physically unable to do the tallest jumps.

"Ah, okay"

She followed the tall elegant man to the tent, it was almost empty this late and the ones who worked there were about to close off for the day but they recognized the two and got them what they wanted. Mr Oswold sat down and sipped at his beer. "So, what do you think of our chances tomorrow?"

Isadora shook her head. "Good? I just fear that Adagio will lose his focus, there are a lot of things to look at in that stadium and he has a tendency to become nervous at the last moment"

Mr Oswold chuckled. "Exactly the same with Silver, he tends to lose focus rather fast. But he does love dressage, I think that horse knows how bloody gorgeous he is"

Isadora had to giggle, "Of course he does, he is posing for the cameras all the time"

Mr Oswold smiled, he was so pretty like that Isadora was sure that he could have seduced a stone! "Yeah, once I had a hard time making him leave the stadium, he was just prancing around trying to impress everybody. And do call me Thor, that Mr Oswold crap gets old, my sponsors can call me that"

She managed to smile and sipped at the beer. It was in fact good, not at all the flat dead liquid she had tasted at similar events earlier. It was a terrible insult to beer to even use the name. The sun had set now and darkness was falling but the huge area was well light, it was needed and she saw that the stable doors were to be closed for the night. Only the grooms were allowed to stay near the stables at night, the horses were extremely valuable and also prone to becoming upset in an unfamiliar stable. She saw that one of the grooms walked by the tent and she waved her hand. "Kenny? Hi!"

He turned on his heel and smiled widely, everybody knew Kenny for he was among the most kind and helpful people imaginable. He was groom for a famous show jumper and Isadora knew him well, they had met several times and Kenny would always do his outmost to help out if there was any sort of problems. "Going to check inn on Tempest?"

He did nod. "Yeah, I am gonna sleep in there tonight, he has been acting up the last few nights, Mr Brown thinks that we may have to buy some extra lights to put over the box, he hates the dark that horse, cannot stand it"

Thor frowned. “So I have heard, that horse is loud! We heard him whinnying the entire night, and was he trying to tear down his whole box?”

Kenny blushed. “He is a goddamn diva is what he is, so spoiled it is a wonder he doesn’t demand having his oats served to him on the finest china. No, I am joking but really, he is a good horse but a pain in the ass too. Too nervous and too aggressive for my liking but what the hey, he does win”

Isadora nodded. “I heard of that groom that got bitten?”

Kenny made a nasty grimace. “Janice yes, she was just walking by the box and that goddamn nag yanked a huge chunk out of her shoulder. Nobody knows why, he just hates people.”

Thor nodded with his head slightly tilted. “He doesn’t hate you?”

Kenny laughed. “No, for I have taught him to respect me, I don’t back down at all and he is a kitten when I am near but nobody else can handle him. I am telling you, that horse is dangerous. If he wasn’t so valuable I would have asked Mr Brown to geld him and break him inn for driving, that tends to make them a bit more mellow.”

Thor finished his beer and wiped off the foam of his chin. “Yeah, a feisty horse may get you lots of medals but also lots of trouble”

Kenny grinned. “No doubt, I better get going before they shut the door, I have placed my sleeping bag in the storage box so I guess it will be an alright night after all, if that horse manages to keep his mouth shut that is"

He winked at Isadora and left and she shook her head. "I really wonder why Mr Brown keeps that animal, he is a bad one"

Thor shrugged. "Is he really? I have seen horses which are way worse, some so bad they should have been put down but where there is money there is a will, in special when the animal is worth more than two million dollars and a heck of a lot more if he goes into stud"

Isadora rolled her eyes. "Yeah, it is insane. I bought Adagio for ten grand, and even that was seen as way too much"

Thor snorted, other words couldn't describe the word. "You have an eye for horseflesh Isadora, you saw the talent and went for it. Not many have that gift these days."

She blushed. "Well, you have Silver Ghost?"

He sighed. "He is of my own breeding Isadora, I have known that bloodline since I was a wee lad, I knew that this one would be special from the day he was born. If you just brought me a handful of nice looking warmblood horses I wouldn't be able to tell the good ones from the lazy ones if my life was on the line"

She laughed. "Oh but I think you would, nobody can train a horse like that and not know all there is to know about them and then some"

It was his time to blush. "I do believe you are right my friend"

He got up. "Time to hit the hay, we'll have to start early tomorrow."

Isadora nodded and finished her beer too, it wasn't very strong but she felt a bit tipsy still, it had to be his presence that triggered that effect. "Indeed we do, did you hear that Rudolph Stevens is gonna be the main judge?"

Thor shuddered and rolled his eyes. "Really? That old bag of bones is as blind as a bat! Well, then it will be anybody's guess who he'll chose"

He petted her on the shoulder. "Have a good night Isadora, See you in the morning"

She nodded and got up too, she had a small room not far from the stable in the building the normal stable workers lived inn. Now they were off duty and so the riders who didn't mind living in a simple manner were placed there together with some of the grooms. Isadora didn't like to be far away from Adagio and she didn't mind the primitive room. She had spent enough time in the luxury suites to know that it didn't matter when the time came and it was her time to do her best. She would rest just as well in a narrow cot as on a wide king size bed. She walked to her room and the stable lights were put out, the lights outside the stables were dimmed and there were guards there too, placed at the entrance to the stable area.

There was a huge fence built around the stables and the security was very good. There were five stables there and each could house a lot of horses, since this was a huge show there were people there competing in almost every equestrian discipline and there were even a competition for women riding in old fashioned side saddles. Now there were some people Isadora could respect, to jump and gallop like that, wearing one of those huge skirts and not even get to have a leg on each side of the horse…She wouldn't even dare to try that on a docile pony, no way. Those women had to have a screw loose.

She found the bed and laid down after having a swift shower and some fruit, she tried not to worry about the next day, she had been in hundreds of competitions but it was always nerve wreaking the night before, what if something happened? What if Adagio was tired? She forced herself to relax and she finally fell asleep, after some tossing and turning.

Isadora was dreaming, it was a dream she always had when she was nervous about something and it wasn't a good one. She was back in England, and she was riding her first professional horse, a grey mare named Turkish Delight, a half Arabian with a bit of a temper and a courage to match it. She was heading for the fifth jump of the course, there were twenty five in all and all very difficult but not all that tall. You just had to hit the hurdle at the right angle. The jump ahead was one she feared, Delight didn't like jumping into water and even to this day she wasn't sure what had really happened.

Had she been too hard and pushed the horse too fast towards the jump? Or hadn't she ridden the horse hard enough and robbed her of confidence? It was hard to say but she still remembered the sickening feeling when she realized that the mare would take off too early. She tried to adjust but it was too late, the horse didn't make it all across the top log and was thrown off balance. Isadora had hit the water and the horse had kicked her right in the chest. She had been knocked out completely but she could remember hearing Delight screaming, an awful piercing sound.

She woke up suddenly, the sound of that scream still in her ears and she shook her head in confusion. It was still dark, why had the nightmare ripped her out of her much needed sleep? Then she realized that she still heard the screams and then a new sound joined them, the flaring sound of a fire alarm. She was up within the blink of an eye, panic rushing through her very being. She didn't care that she was in her knickers and bra, she got a pair of slippers on and ran outside. She screamed in shock, the stable was burning, thick black smoke hanging over the area and why the hell hadn't the alarms gone off before? She ran, without thinking. Adagio was in there and she had to save him.

The door was locked, with a chain?! But there was a side door there somewhere and she ran, tore it open. Horses were screaming and she heard faint sirens, the fair-grounds had its own fire brigade, they were coming. The roof was burning, debris was raining down and the smoke was thick and black, where was Adagio? She had to find him, she would never forgive herself if she let her horse die. She stumbled, the smoke was burning in her lungs and she leaned against the wall. Where was she? She had to think, he had to be on the other side of the wide corridor and to the left. She coughed and fought her way forth, she was reaching for a water bucket to throw over herself when something suddenly struck her on the head and the world did spin before her eyes before it became black. Her last thought was that she couldn't lose Adagio too, not when she already had lost Delight.

Isadora opened her eyes slowly, she was feeling as if she had been run over by a truck and her chest hurt. There was a white roof above her and she heard a lot of bipping machines and …a hospital? Oh God no, Adagio!! She tried to sit up and a hand was suddenly on her shoulder. It was Linda, and she had been crying, her eyes were red and swollen and she had some nasty burns on her cheeks and her hair was singed, she looked terrible. "Linda?!"

The groom nodded. "Yes, it is me, oh I am so sorry Isadora"

She felt her heart almost stopping in her chest. "Adagio?"

Linda swallowed. "Is alive, for now. They managed to get him out, but he has inhaled a lot of smoke, the vets don't know yet if he will make it and if he does…he won't be able to compete again Isadora"

Isadora felt as if in a vacuum. "What happened?"

Linda looked down. "The fire brigade found you and pulled you out, it was in the nick of time!"

Isadora swallowed hard, her throat was raw and sore and her chest did sting like mad. "The doors, they were chained stuck… and the fire alarm…"

Linda nodded. "Yes, the fire brigade just drove the truck through the doors, to open them. Somebody…"

She was choking. “Somebody started the fire on purpose Isadora. The fire alarm was disabled all over the fair ground. But this one stable has an extra system because of the closed room at the top of the stable, where they keep pregnant mares. So it went off still. “

Isadora went silent for a few seconds. Arson? No, it couldn’t be… Who would do something so terrible…

Linda sobbed. “Oh Isadora, we lost many horses, and Kenny is dead”

Isadora just stared at her, remembered that Kenny was to stay in the stable that night. “What?”

Linda nodded. “He was found near the fire alarm button, had probably tried to trigger it, but he died before he could make it work again.”

Isadora felt as if she was still in a nightmare. “The smoke?”

Linda sighed, her eyes were distant. “No, he was stabbed Isadora, in the back. The person behind this probably didn’t want anybody to trigger the alarm.”

Isadora let out a wail. “Which…which horses…”

Linda closed her eyes. “Mr Berner did lose two horses he had brought over to sell, and nineteen of the other competitors did lose their horses….”

Her voice broke, she was almost choking. “And Mr Oswold lost Silver Ghost.”

She sobbed. “The bastard lit also another stable on fire, there they didn’t manage to save even one horse, thirty animals were killed there”

Isadora felt faint, light headed. It couldn’t be true. No, it was a dream, a horrible dream, she shouldn’t have had that beer. She wanted to pinch her arm but saw those bandages and felt the pain and realized that it was real and not some horrible nightmare. She screamed, and Linda embraced her gently, the girl was trembling. “At least ten grooms are hurt, two by horses and eight by falling debris and smoke. It is…it is a mess”

Isadora stared at her, wild eyed. “How long have I been here?”

Linda took a deep breath. “Two whole days, they feared that you had such severe damages to your lungs they would have to intubate you but you pulled through”

The groom sighed. “The police are all over the place now, since Kenny was killed it is a homicide investigation and there are hundreds of people who are so pissed they are spitting fire, they demand to know who killed several of the best show horses in the world. And the insurance companies are sweating blood, if they have to pay for this they will lose a lot, almost everything I bet.”

Isadora blinked. Some of the horses were insured for many millions of dollars, if they were lost then it would indeed be a terrible blow to the companies.

A nurse entered the room, she did look friendly enough and smiled. “How do you feel Ms Singer?”

Isadora swallowed. “Like shit”

The nurse smiled even wider. “No wonder, you were mad to go inside of a burning stable like that, you must know that?”

Isadora sighed “Yes, I do, now! All I could think about was saving my horse”

The nurse nodded. “I understand, I would have done the same thing you know. Are you in pain?”

Isadora shook her head. “Not much no, I feel it but I have felt worse”

The nurse sat down and checked the monitors. “You are tougher than old nails girl”

Isadora tried to smile. “Well, I am an equestrian, we need to be tougher than flint”

The nurse took a stethoscope and listened “That is very true miss. Your heartbeat is good now, steady. It was rather unstable when they brought you inn. You were in a terrible state.”

Isadora made a grimace. “Yeah, I guess. How long do I have to stay?”

The nurse shrugged. “I have to ask the doctors, but at least a week”

Isadora gasped. “No way, I cannot be here. I need to be with Adagio, and and…”

The nurse touched her hand gently. “I am sorry Ma’am, but you cannot leave yet. You have some head trauma and your skin was badly scorched too in places, you were hit by burning debris.”

Linda managed to smile, faintly. “I will keep an eye on him and call you the moment there is a change. Do not worry, the insurance is paying for the treatment”

Isadora sobbed. “Yes, but…I should be there, for him”

Linda nodded slowly. “I know, but you have to get well, for Adagio. Please?”

Isadora felt how the salty tears did sting her skin, it really had been a matter of moments before she too would have succumbed to the heat. “Alright but call me if something happens, no matter when”

Linda nodded and leaned over, kissed her on the brow gently. “I promise Isadora, I will.”

Linda got up and left, wiping her face discretely.

Isadora just laid there, staring at the ceiling, trying to understand what had happened. Then she slowly drifted off, due to her injuries and the drugs she had been given.

The next time she woke up there was a stranger sitting by her bed, he was wearing a rather worn jacket and his face was sympathetic and yet it had a sort of raggedness to it. He smiled at her. “Ms Singer, I am chief investigator Jason Armaggio, I work with the local police to solve this case”

Isadora managed to sit up, but it hurt like hell. “Oh yes, Kenny…”

The investigator nodded solemnly. “It was obvious that he was killed by someone who didn’t want any witnesses. When you entered, did you see anybody?”

Isadora shook her head. “No, there could have been a whole army in there though, I couldn’t see more than a few feet in all that smoke. And then I think I was hit by some debris?”

The investigator made a grimace. “Ah not quite so Ms Singer, you were knocked out by somebody. Probably the culprit”

She blinked. “But…how? The heat…the smoke…”

Mr Armaggio sighed. “Yes, the culprit was prepared, probably wearing a full fireman’s gear, with oxygen and all. And slipped out during the chaos, there were firefighters running everywhere and grooms and others too. He left a wrench next to you, probably what he used to strike you down”

Isadora felt nauseous, somebody had tried to kill her. It was a horrible shock. “Oh God!”

The investigator tried to smile. “Still, you were found, and you are alive. We are doing our best to solve this”

Isadora felt tears flowing down her cheeks again. “You have to catch this bastard, promise you will”

Jason got up and touched her hand. “I do, I won’t rest until that monster is caught, somebody able to harm such wonderful creatures is no human”

Isadora didn’t find any more words, she just allowed herself to fall back to sleep, the nurses were there and changed bandages and washed her but she didn't notice. The doctors kept her under for as much time as possible, to make sure her skin would heal.

She was awake when the nurse told her she had a guest. At first she was sure it was Linda but it was Thor. He looked as splendid as always but she saw that his eyes were red and she remembered that he had lost his horse. Her heart sank within her chest. "Mr Oswold?"

He sat down, eyes on the floor. "Isadora....I...I just wanted to check inn on you. I spoke to Linda, you were so brave, and so very stupid"

She swallowed hard. "Yes, I know. I am so sorry for your loss"

Thor heaved for air. "I loved that horse like a brother, he was family."

She nodded, she had seen the incredible bond between the two of them. He lifted his head again, the long silky blond hair like a curtain, covering some of his face. "I am so glad I stayed at the hotel, if I had been living anywhere near the stable I would have tried to do what you did and probably died"

Isadora heard the heartbreak in his voice and sympathy filled her very being. "You couldn't have saved him Thor, whoever was in there killed Kenny, he would have killed you too"

Thor nodded. "I have spoken to the investigator, they have several theories but I do not agree with them. I and Brent have been discussing it a lot."

She frowned. "Oh, Brent. What was wrong with Moon?"

Thor made a small smile. "Some sort of stomach ache, it did only last for a couple of hours but before they could return to the stable…well, you know. But Brent is devastated still, good horses did die, and Mr Berner is a broken man now. "

Isadora took a deep breath. "So, what are the theories?"

Thor did sit back in the chair, turned the hat he had been wearing in his hands. "Insurance fraud. Others claim that it is people who protest against the use of horses for sports who is behind it all. Another funny idea is that somebody wanted to get rid of the competition"

Isadora coughed and her throat did sting like mad. "What?"

He nodded. "You heard me right, and then we have the idea that this was just an arsonist, somebody who gets off on watching things burn"

Isadora tried to calm herself. "I don't believe that"

Thor smiled. "Neither do I, and by the way, Anna has gone missing"

She froze. "Moon's groom?"

Thor took a deep breath and nodded. "None other, and she would never just leave that mare, the investigator is sure something has happened to her but what? She is nowhere to be found"

Isadora had to swallow hard. "They have searched through the stable?"

Thor nodded. "Yes, and removed the…bodies. The entire area was sealed off, there were technicians all over the place"

Isadora took a deep breath, steadied herself. “Have you spoken to that investigator Jason…what was his last name?”

Thor had to grin. “Yes, Mr Armaggio, a decent chap but he doesn’t know a darn thing about horses nor the equestrian industry”

Isadora had to grin too, how could you not when that drop dead gorgeous man was sitting this close. “He is a cop, most of them don’t know the front end from the back end of a horse”

Thor snickered. “Well, I have met some who were amazing on horseback, but then we speak of rather rural areas where you may have to chase someone on horseback”

Isadora knew that Thor owned his own ranch somewhere west and that it was very large. It wouldn’t surprise her at all if it all was a bit “wild west” in that area still. Thor looked down. “There will be a memorial service tomorrow, outside of the fairgrounds. Everybody loved Kenny and the priest is kind enough to say some words also about the horses which were lost”

Isadora blinked and had to swallow hard. “That is kind of him, some don’t see animals as anything but things”

Thor nodded and his face was sad again . “Yes, but this is a good man, I think he owns horses too.”

She did change her position slightly. “I will try to be there, if the doctors do allow it”

Thor tilted his head. “Is that very smart of you?”

She snorted. “Probably not but try to keep me away. I want to be there, to pay my respects. There were thirty lost in that other stable?”

Thor nodded. "Yes, and the fire there started after the one in our stable so the culprit was still there when chaos erupted. I wish I could grasp that bastard and do things to him no human ought to"

Isadora felt a sting of ice cold rage. "Then you will have to line up, I am in front of you in that queue. "

Thor sighed. "Most of the newspaper do speak only of the monetary value of the horses lost, they don't speak of the heartbreak and sorrow of the riders and grooms. I have seen more grown men cry over the last days than ever before in my life. I have cried to, I am not ashamed to admit it. Brent didn't lose his horse but he was bawling still, anyone fond of animals would"

Isadora nodded and had to cough. She still had the taste of smoke in her mouth and she had realized that her face still was red and sore. It made her feel embarrassed. Thor reached out and gently pushed a strand of her hair out of the way, she stared at him, it was a rather intimate gesture and not at all typical for him. "Pardon me, but I was just tempted. "

She had to blush even deeper and he smiled, got back up. "Then I guess I will see you tomorrow?"

She tried to look calm and collected, but her heart was racing. "Yes, I hope so"

He put his hat back on and winked and she laid there, feeling a sort of disbelief. It had to be the grief, he couldn't really be interested? No, it was just that they were in the same boat so to speak. Even if Adagio survived he wouldn't be able to compete again, they were both horseless now.

Isadora insisted on participating at the memorial and the doctors were at first adamant that she had to stay there but in the end they budged. But she had to be in a wheel chair and wear an oxygen mask and cover her skin too. It made her feel a bit like the phantom of the opera but she felt that she couldn't just ignore that voice within that told her to show up. She owed it to them all.

The morning came with light rain and a grey sky and it was perfect really. An ambulance drove her off to the ceremony, she felt a bit like an odd animal as she was pushed towards the crowd by Linda who came to meet her. The girl was wearing black and looked rather classy for once. Brent and Thor came to meet her too and they went to the front of the crowd together. There were hundreds of people there and all wore black and it did look like a funeral, and perhaps it was one, just not in the ordinary manner. The priest spoke a lot, he told about Kenny and his kindness and the dead horses were also mentioned as if they had been people. There were already plans for the erection of a huge statue by the stables, as a memorial to those lost. The equestrian society had started a campaign to fund it and they had already received enough money for several massive statues.

Brent stood there and looked sombre and Thor was a bit pale, he also wore black and was so majestic many of the reporters who had gathered there were beside themselves with enthusiasm. The pictures would be exquisite. Isadora knew that she was close to un - recognizable due to her bandages and she was glad, she didn't want to answer any questions, not now. She just sat there, listening and sobbing quietly and she wasn't the only one, most there were tearing up and now she noticed that there was a tethering post behind the stand where the priest finished his speeches. It was covered with halters, singed and half burned ones and the sight sent her stomach churning. Thor placed a hand on her shoulder, very gently. "Are you alright?"

She nodded. "Yes, it's just…Those halters…"

He sighed. "Yes, I have seen them, some of the grooms removed them from the dead horses, and hung them there, I bet they wanted to make it more real to the public"

Isadora was fighting for air and her chest felt as if an elephant was kneeling on it. "I…I cannot stand it, I have to…get out of here"

Thor grasped the back of the wheelchair and turned her around, started pushing her away from the sight and Brent joined them. He was mumbling something and Isadora didn't hear it but she was rather sure it was nothing nice. They had almost made it back to the ambulance when Isadora saw that Mr Berner came walking towards them. She was shocked by the sight. She had seen the old man just a few months ago and he had been such an image of a vigorous and fit elderly person. He was in his eighties but looked as if he was just in his early sixties and she had admired his brisk vitality. Now he looked his age, he used a cane and his eyes were sunken and had lost their intensity. He was suddenly an old man and he stopped next to them and lifted a hand to his hat in a polite gesture. "Ms Singer, Mr Brewster, Mr Oswold"

Brent did nod back. “Mr Berner, my heartfelt condolences”

The old man tried to smile, but the smile faltered, the eyes got watery and he was leaning heavily on the stick. “My friends, I have been through a lot in my life, but never something like this, I pray to God above that the one behind this will be caught soon. If he isn’t I am willing to put out a reward, a hundred grand to the one who brings that beast to justice”

Isadora gasped and felt shocked to the core. “That is a lot of money, you will be overrun by all sorts of wackos”

Mr Berner grunted. “Maybe, but I lost more than a couple of horses Ms Singer, I lost my hope, my soul. The filly which died…she was the granddaughter of my precious Velveteen Wonder and her spitting image. I had such high hopes for her, she could have become a world champion, easily”

Isadora swallowed hard. “I am so sorry to hear that, I have heard of Velveteen, she was unique. And the other horse you lost?”

He sighed and Mr Brewster offered the old man his arm, Mr Berner accepted. Previously he would never have shown such weakness, he was falling apart, that was the truth of it. “An old friend of mine, Gerard’s folly. A lead pony, twenty years of age and ready for retirement, I had hoped to sell him to some aspiring young rider, he was an excellent teacher”

Thor frowned, his eyes curious. “Why selling him? He sounds like the sort of horse you need in a large stable, to keep the youngsters calm.”

Mr Berner nodded, "Yes, he often made himself useful that way, he would teach the yearlings manners for sure. But my old stable master Mr Dickens had a heart attack three months ago and the new one I hired is an excellent worker and very dedicated and filled with knowledge but he and old Folly never saw eye to eye. I had to let him go, the horse just couldn't stand the man"

Isadora stared at the old man. "Really? That is odd, did the other horses react that way?"

Mr Berner sighed. "No, it was just Folly, he was a bit odd in his old age, and Mr Hall was never anything but gentle and kind to the old chap but Folly obviously decided that he hated him, could be that he missed Mr Dickens. Horses are odd creatures at times"

He coughed. "I lost both him and Velveteen Darkness and if I ever have wished for someone to burn in hell it is the person behind this"

He wiped his eyes with his handkerchief. "I am just grateful that Crested Moon was spared"

He let go of Brent's arm and walked off, not even looking back and Thor sighed and looked very sad indeed. "There walks a broken man"

Brent nodded. "He has lost his spark, his hope. He is making a mistake though, a reward like that will most certainly bring all the nutcases out of the darkness and into the light."

Thor nodded. "And many of the others here will be eager to add to the reward to, many are genuinely pissed off"

Isadora looked down, she felt conflicted. A part of her wanted to applaud what Mr Berner was doing, the more sensible part of her was far less enthusiastic. Brent was right, this could turn into a witch hunt of epic proportions. She just hoped that the police found the culprit before the equine society did, she wouldn't bet that a lynching was impossible.

She was back at the ambulance and ready to say goodbye to Thor and Brent when her phone rang, it was a number she didn't know but her phone did identify it as the animal hospital. She felt her heart sink, and the two men saw her expression and Thor did snatch the phone from her. "Yes?"

Isadora could hear a faint female voice, it was shivering and Thor hurried to present himself as a friend of Isadora. Then there was some shouting in the background and the female voice came back, Isadora didn't hear the words but the tone of the voice told her everything. She broke down into tears and Thor ended the call and went down on his haunches, embraced her gently. "I am so so sorry Isadora, it was the vet. Adagio has collapsed, it is most likely his heart. They just ended it, he was suffering"

Isadora let out a wail and Thor rocked her in his arms, he sent a glance filled with despair at Brent who made a grimace. "I am terribly sorry to hear that Ms Singer, I was a great admirer of Adagio, he was magnificent. If I can do anything to help…"

Isadora just wailed and Thor took a deep breath. "Isadora, this may sound heartless but what do you want them to do with the body?"

She blinked, it was unreal, it couldn't be true. "I…I want him buried back home? Is it even possible?"

Brent snapped his fingers. "It is, I will make it happen. I will make some calls, he will rest where he does belong, do not worry Isadora, it will be organized."

She sobbed. "My…my uncle does run the stable when I am away, he…he will know where to dig the grave…"

She grasped the phone and found the number, she didn't have the strength to make the call and Brent took the phone and walked off to notify the man of the tragedy. Thor still held her, and it felt strangely comforting. He smelled of leather and horse and something almost woodsy and she inhaled the scent, feeling oddly protected. He sighed deeply. "I have already sent the body of Silver Ghost to be buried back home, most of the dead horses were burned, the bodies couldn't be used for anything and digging a grave for that many large animals would have been impossible"

Isadora sobbed. "It is so undignified"

Thor nodded. "Yes, it was, but rest assured that it will end"

He sent Brent a smile as he returned with Isadora's phone. "I will go with her, she shouldn't be alone now. You can tag along if you like?"

Brent shook his head. "I appreciate the offer but Anna is still missing and Crested Moon is very skittish now, she has been placed in a smaller stable and she doesn't like it there. I have to go and check upon her"

Thor smiled faintly. “Do that, and if you hear anything, give us a call?”

Brent nodded and took Thor’s hand. “I will, and thanks”

Thor smiled and just shrugged and Brent walked off. Isadora swallowed hard. “Thanks for what?”

Thor tilted his head. “I did him a favour yesterday, just a small one. But nevermind, I don’t think you ought to go back to the hospital, it is too depressing. I have a suite at the hotel, and there is spare room”

Isadora gaped. “Really, ah…but I need treatment and…”

Thor smiled. “Yes, but I can organize it so the nurses come to you, I bet you will feel way better in a more normal room? Those sterile hospital rooms make me go insane, and I bet they do the same to you right?”

She blushed and had to admit that it did sound tempting. The room she had been inn for many days now was terribly boring, the TV didn’t work and it was both too clean and too alien for her. “I do thank you but we have to get the permission of the doctors first”

He winked at her and it made her pulse go nuts. “I can fix that, don’t worry”

Half an hour later they were delivered by the hotel Thor lived at, it was one of the best in the city and very elegant and they had gotten all the equipment Isadora needed. A nurse would show up twice a day and check on her and Isadora was rather sure that Thor had paid off the doctors to allow her to stay there with him. Rumours said that he was filthy rich but now she saw that there could be some truth to it, the suite was grand and luxurious and at the same time not overly gaudy. It had class and he fit inn there like he was born to be living in such expensive places. Isadora still felt terribly upset and when they were inside he crouched down and embraced her again. “I know you would want to see Adagio but don’t, remember him as he was. Nobody ought to see their beloved horse laying there like a lump of dead meat”

She suddenly remembered Delight and burst into tears again, wailing with barely any sound and he started to hum softly, stroking her back gently. “You remember don’t you? I have heard about your accident”

She managed to nod. “Yes…she…”

He sighed deeply. “I saw those pictures, today they may have saved her but ten years ago? Not possible, they wouldn’t have been able to keep her alive for long enough to fix those tendons. She would have succumbed to it eventually, a fracture like that is almost always lethal to a horse. I am impressed that you made it back into the saddle though”

Isadora tried to control herself. “I had to, riding is my life”

Thor let go of her and smiled. “Says everybody bitten by that bug. I learned how to ride before I learned how to walk. But you are still affected by it?”

Isadora swallowed the bitterness. The fall had not only torn several tendons in Delight’s left hind leg and fractured her right shoulder, it had also resulted in Isadora breaking her pelvis in three places, her sternum in two and her right femur and ankle. She had spent months in rehab and her pelvis would still hurt at times. It wasn't as flexible as it ought to be anymore. She had perhaps ten years of riding left, then she would simply be too stiff to compete anymore.

"Yes, I have learned to appreciate each day, one ride will be my last"

He shook his head. "Too bad, you have a rare talent"

She looked down, her hands were grasping the blankets as if she was trying to strangle them. "I may be talented but without a horse like Adagio I will never reach the top. Finding a new horse like him and training it will be close to impossible, I simply doesn't have the time anymore."

Thor stroked her hair gently. "Don't say that, I will keep an eye open. I know many breeders and I am sure there is a horse out there born just for you."

She had to laugh, a small insecure laughter. "Says the man who owns like a hundred horses?"

Thor grinned, there as a small devil playing within those eyes. "Yeah, but you are not even close, it is more like five hundred"

She gasped. "Are you nuts? Five hundred?!"

He nodded. "I do have a sanctuary on my farm, most are retired show horses and racers but I do also have a lot of mustangs and discarded carriage horses."

She had to blink, she hadn't known that about him. He got up. "Are you hungry?"

She nodded and felt that she ought to lay down. The day had been a long one at least emotionally, and one with a lot of emotional stress. She pulled herself over into the couch, her legs could barely carry her yet and she felt terribly weak. Thor called for room service and after a while a servant came with a trolley filled with the most delicious chicken dish she had ever tasted. And the wine which came to it was perfect too. She felt embarrassed, she was no pauper by any means but Thor was most definitely a man who knew class and quality, and how to behave without flaunting his wealth. She ought to pay him back for this, somehow.

She finished eating and stared at him. "The favour you did for Brent, what was it?"

He just shrugged. "Why do you ask?"

She frowned. "I want to know for sure what sort of a man you are?"

He sighed again and put down his fork, he made a grimace. "I am sure you know that Brent is gay?"

She nodded. "The best known secret of the equestrian community yes"

Thor looked as if he had tasted something foul. "Yeah, we have no problem with that at all, most of the riders don't give a damn about these things. He has a boyfriend and they are just a match made in heaven. But Brent has an aunt who owns the entire family business and she cannot be told that he is the way he is. She is extremely anti anything which isn't arch conservative and backwards and she will disown him if she finds out"

Isadora had to gape, such attitudes were hard to understand but she knew they were out there. "Really?!"

Thor nodded. "Yes, and there has been this one reporter who managed to snatch a snapshot of him and Joel together, in an intimate setting"

Isadora swallowed. "You made it go away didn't you?"

Thor grinned, a very devious grin. "I know people you see, who know people. That reporter has deleted those images and he won't bother Brent again, ever."

She had to snicker. "Did you threaten to crush his knees like in the old gangster movies?"

Thor shook his head. "Heck no, I am no barbarian. It is just that a certain reporter has failed to report a huge part of his income to the tax authorities, over the last five years. They would be very grateful if somebody was to tip them…."

She could barely believe it. "Oh my God Thor, you are devious"

He cocked his head and was so charming she was sure he could have melted a glacier. "Why thank you ma'am, I am doing my best"

She giggled and he reached out and let a finger slide along her cheek, the gesture and touch made her gasp and she didn't really know what to say and do. He did lean inn a bit closer and whispered to her. "Isadora…"

She was sure that he was going to kiss her when the doorbell rung and she jumped and cursed the person outside of the door to heck and back. “Enter”

Thor was back on his feet, looking as calm as can be. The door did open and Linda walked in, she was still in black and she was weeping. Isadora felt her heart drop, Linda had loved Adagio too and she had almost forgotten about her! She felt like the worst person ever!

Linda fell to her knees next to the couch. “Oh Isa, I am so sorry. I don’t know what to say”

Isadora took her hand. “I know sweetheart, I know. I feel the same way. They are gonna send him back home, to Springwell. He will rest next to Delight”

Linda nodded. “I…I am sorry, but…I…sorry for the pun but I need to get back into the saddle if you know what I mean?”

Isadora frowned. “Yes?”

Linda swallowed, she was snotty and sniffled. “Mrs Jackson called me just half an hour ago. She asked if I could work for her for a while. Damon is among the injured grooms and Secretive is a very high strung horse and needs someone calm”

Isadora sighed. Of course, Linda needed a job, she wasn’t working for free after all and was sought after. She was skilled and experienced. She took a deep breath. “That is alright dear, do take the job. You need it after all. And Mrs Jackson will be very grateful, not everybody can handle that horse”

Linda did bite her lower lip. “Are you sure? I feel as if I am letting you down Isa, I would never even consider this if…”

Isadora leaned over and hugged the girl. “I know, but the facts are the facts. I am horseless right now and have no use for a groom and you are perfectly allowed to seek a new job. Go, don’t feel guilty. I do really feel happy for you. Mrs Jackson is a rising star and you will become very appreciated. Nobody handles feisty horses like you do.”

Linda sobbed and hugged her back and squeezed Isadora’s hand. “Thank you, thank you so much!”

She got up and wiped her eyes, she did look terrible with mascara smeared all over her face. “I am so grateful Isa, just let me know if there is anything and if you get back I want to come back to work for you”

Isadora felt a bit moved. “Thank you Linda, I will remember that. Do me a favour, keep your eyes and ears open, there could be that somebody knows something regarding the fire”

Linda smiled, but they saw that she was close to tears again. “Will do, I promise.”

She shook Isadora’s hand again and nodded to Thor and then she left. Isadora was left feeling oddly light headed. Linda had always been there when Isadora’s career was on the rise, it would be odd not having her there. Thor sat down next to her. “Are you alright?”

Isadora wiped her eyes, damnation, it seemed as if crying was all she had done over the last days. “Yes, it is just…it is so much to digest. I still feel as if I am in a nightmare. I never imagined that I would lose Adagio, not like that"

Thor sighed softly and placed an arm around her shoulders, very gently and in a manner which was only compassionate. "I know the feeling. "

She squinted. "You have lost a horse before too?"

He nodded and his eyes were a bit distant. "Yes, not a show horse or some valuable stud but a friend, a wild horse I came to know at my ranch. He didn't have a name but he taught me all I know now about how horses think and act. "

Isadora swallowed. "A mustang?"

He smiled, a glimpse of melancholy in his eyes. "Yes, a large dun stallion, a band leader. He had five mares and some foals and I would seek them out ever so often and just sit there and watch them for hours. It was so peaceful seeing them living their lives, the way horses are supposed to live."

Isadora could almost see it, and she felt the warmth in his voice and knew that he had a heart larger than most others. At least when it came to animals. And she did adore him for it. "How did you lose him?"

Her voice was low, she didn't want to cause him distress but he smiled, a sad swift smile. "A thunderstorm, the whole band had sought refuge in a small holt of trees and a bolt struck the tallest tree there. The whole band died, each and every one. I was heartbroken but then again, he died where he lived, free. He could have been among those poor things which are rounded up each year and sent off to the slaughterhouses of Canada or Mexico"

Isadora frowned. "Can they do that on your ranch?"

Thor shook his head. "No, my land is off limits to the authorities and I am buying more land each year, I plan on making it a sanctuary for all sorts of wildlife in the end"

Isadora nodded. It did sound like a grand plan, and a noble one.

There was another knock on the door and this time it was the nurse, Isadora knew this one well by now and the woman swiftly checked her bandages and declared that they could come off the next day and that Isadora was well enough to take a bath the next morning. The nurse would return at half past eight to help her and Isadora swallowed a small cry of relief, she felt like a cave dweller by now, her hair greasy and heavy and her skin felt as if it was covered with sooth still.

Thor had turned on the TV as Isadora and the nurse spoke and when the woman left Isadora was placed in the couch again, to watch a movie. She found that she and Thor had the exact same taste in movies, silly over the top comedies and disaster movies and they sat there and laughed and had fun for a few hours. She oddly enough felt as if she had known him for a lifetime and couldn't even remember when she first saw him. Nobody really knew that much about him, except from the fact that he was single and that he owned a large ranch. When the movie was over it was getting late and Isadora was helped to bed by a very careful Thor who even let the door to her room stand ajar in case she needed something. She hadn't felt that pampered since she was a kid.

The next morning she slept until the nurse was due to return and had to get up in a hurry, feeling dozy and confused and she looked like a train wreck. Her hair was standing on end and she had pillow impressions on her face and the pyjamas she had been wearing were more wrinkled than a litter of Shar Pei puppies. And Thor smiled at her and greeted her as if she was some vision of feminine beauty and grace. She was sure that she could have been transformed into something the size of a hippo over the night and he would still have been acting this way. That man had been raised just the right way, no doubt about it.

The nurse came right on time and Isadora had her bandages removed, she hadn't really suffered that much of burn injuries as much as smoke inhalation but some debris had fallen onto her as she laid unconscious, Getting rid of the bandages felt like returning to her own body, and having a bath was even better. The nurse spent a long time washing her hair and when Isadora was done she was a new person. It felt like rebirth, like becoming someone new. Someone, probably one of the grooms, had been kind enough to bring her stuff from the room by the stables and she found some clean clothes and suddenly life was good again. It wasn't perfect but she felt more confident and Thor grinned at her as she emerged from her room. "Now there is the Isadora Singer I have come to know"

Isadora blushed and she almost giggled but she had to admit that with her hair clean and braided and some light make up she looked a billion times better. “Thank you”

He did a wide gesture. “I have taken the opportunity to order us a light breakfast, I hope that is okay?”

She took a deep breath, normally she would have been in the stable by now and her breakfast usually consisted of a few bananas and a kit kat, eaten on the run so to speak. A real breakfast was a rare treat and she had to smile, a sort of sad smile. There was a reason why the riders were so fit, nobody had time to sit down and eat. The breakfast was in no manner light, there were everything from toast to scrambled eggs and bacon and beans and some stuff she didn’t even recognize but it was all so very tasty and she wondered if all the guests of this hotel were that privileged or if it was just those who rented the suites. Thor would eat in silence, he was reading the newspapers on his laptop and made a frown, he turned it so Isadora could see. It was a headline which did make her gape and swallow hard. It said with huge bold letters. “More than thirty prize winners killed in insurance fraud”

She stared at him. “How dare they?”

Thor sighed. “They want headlines, and readers. The truth is just an inconvenience in their eyes, something which can go fuck itself. I bet most people do believe it too, that somebody set the stables on fire to collect the insurance money for their horse”

Isadora did almost growl. “In that case they are morons! Nobody would do that, do they even know how much time and dedication we spend on our animals?! I doubt it!!”

Thor nodded, there was a hint of a smirk on his face. “Easy there Isa, whoa! You are stunning when you are angry but remember, you were injured. No need to push yourself”

She blushed again. “But I mean it, goddamn it! We cannot let them slander the name of our society, there are so many good people out there”

Thor tilted his head and nodded slowly, his expression one of hidden anger. “And a few rotten apples, but they usually flush themselves out in time”

Isadora bit into an apple and found that it was both crispy and sweet, just the way she favoured apples. “Have you come across those?”

Thor pushed his plate aside, he had eaten a massive amount of food but you could tell that he was used to hard work for the t shirt he wore revealed that he was both lean and ripped, in just the right manner. Stable work will do that to you. “Yeah, a few times. I worked as a stable designer for a couple of years, before I became a professional eventer, and one stable I did visit. Oh holy bejeezes how I wanted to nail the owner to a wall with a hayfork”

Isadora leaned a bit forward, he had probably experienced a lot and she was curious. “Really? What was the problem?”

He grimaced and closed the laptop, his eyes were a bit hard. “It was a stable for show horses, Tennessee Walkers.”

She felt a bit of a sickening feeling in her guts. “Soring?”

He nodded. “Yep, the worst kind. I saw horses with more than a dozen nails hammered into their hooves, and some with carbolic acid smeared onto their fetlocks. Those poor animals were in agony, just so they would lift their legs high and look completely ridiculous while doing it, like crippled frogs!”

Isadora blinked. “What did you do?”

Thor grinned, a very nasty grin. “I stayed calm and said that yes, I could redesign the stable and the price would be so and so, way higher than normal. And then I called every other person I knew in the business and told them what I had seen. Nobody wanted to work for that piece of scum after that”

She had to laugh. “Devious again, but you didn’t do anything to the man?”

He shook his head. “Nope, not that time. But I spend some time at a police station once, because of a bastard I had the privilege of beating.”

She had to look at him again, there was a dark fire burning in the gaze and she realized that he was capable of actually harming others, if he had to. The kindest hearts may harbour the greatest fury. “Really?”

He lifted his feet up onto a bench and grinned. “I was just finished at college, in my early twenties. And I had started running the farm already, my father insisted that I learned what responsibility was. One of the guys we hired was somewhat shady, he would work and did obey but there just was something about him I didn't like, he was simply too low key if you catch my drift? It was rather obvious that he was hiding something"

Isadora moved the food out of the way, leaned her elbows onto the table. "Do tell"

Thor sent her a grin, his eyes were glittering. "I think that the good lady do enjoy hearing of the demise of scum right?"

She nodded. "It never gets old now does it. To know that justice has been served"

Thor reached over and caressed her hand swiftly. "That is good"

He leaned back again and cocked his head, the long silky hair was almost glowing in the sunlight streaming inn from the large windows. "I kept an eye on the guy, and lo and behold, he revealed himself in time."

Isadora held her breath. "What did he do?"

Thor let out a grunt of disgust and looked down, he made a grimace. "The ranch is rather large Isadora, with many buildings and we do have a housekeeper. Mrs Scott, she is a widow, her husband died in an accident at a building site six years before she started working for us. She had a kid, a seven year old daughter"

Isadora gaped. "Oh no, don't tell me that the creep…"

Thor closed his eyes, he sounded almost tired. "Yes, I caught him, in an abandoned hay barn. He had lured the kid over to the place, and had bound and gagged her and had a very good time. But that didn't last"

Isadora felt a bit nauseous, the idea of somebody abusing a child in that manner was sickening. "What did you do…"

Thor smiled, but the smile didn't reach his eyes. They were ice cold. "We have to work a bit like vets at times, be able to fix all sorts of stuff for the vet can be far away. So we have equipment you may say. I beat the crap out of him with a horse whip, then I tied him up and went to work with a pair of castration thongs"

Isadora squealed, she knew those tools. They were used to castrate bulls, and they did crush the blood supply to the testicles, making them atrophy and die. It was bloodless but very efficient and way more humane than the ordinary rubber band method. "Oh God, that was…deserved"

Thor nodded, his smile was still ice cold. "The guy pressed charges, but the evidence was against him and the sheriff questioned me of course but shook my hand afterwards and the guy spent some years in jail. He had done the same thing earlier, the feds were after him and he had given us a fake name. But jail time was not all he got, the deputy visited me a year after and told me that the bastard had become the lady boy of some huge thug and was rented out to everybody in the prison, the guards included. I guess you can say it was well deserved"

She had to laugh, a rather incredulous laughter. "God, there is justice in the world. But the kid?"

Thor made a grimace again, "Had severe injuries, and lost a lot of blood. I am so sorry I didn't get there earlier but the bastard did sneak off and I had forgotten all about that barn. The doctors stitched her up again though and she is alright now, a very smart young lady. The shrinks did a good job working with her"

Isadora nodded. "That is good"

Thor lifted a jar of orange juice. "If you are done eating I will ask the room service to remove the food?"

She nodded and Thor was on his way to the phone when there was a knock on the door. He turned on his heels and opened it and it was Brent and Mr Armaggio, both looked a bit eager and Brent almost ran into the room. "Thor, Isadora, they have found Anna"

Thor went quiet and Isadora swallowed slowly, her gut dropped, the expression on Brent's face told her everything. "She is dead?"

He nodded and both he and the investigator sat down, Jason spun his hat between his hands, he looked as if he didn't really know what to do. "Yes, they found her body in a sewer outside of the city this morning, very badly burned but the dental records did identify her"

Brent swallowed hard and Isadora saw tears on his cheeks. "She…she had hidden something…"

Thor stared at them, the eyes were like blue lasers there and then. "What?"

Brent took a huge gulp of air. "When they retrieved the body they found that she had worn pants which were a bit too long, she had just folded the legs double a few times. And in the fold on her left leg…"

Brent reached into his pocket and retrieved an object. It was an ampoule, made from glass. The old fashioned type doctors and vets used before plastic became the norm. It contained a sort of brownish liquid and it did look rather old. “This”

Thor took it carefully, stared at it with wide eyes. “Is it…”

Brent nodded. “It is, no vet uses this anymore but it was very popular for a while, in the thirties and forties that is”

Isadora stared at them, eyes wandering from one to the other. “What the heck is it? Tell me?”

Brent smiled, his eyes were sad and also a bit confused. “It is a medicine used against colic, very efficient too if the horse do have colic. If it hasn’t then well, it will cause stomach cramps”

Isadora had to take two deep breaths. “What Crested Moon had?”

Brent nodded. “Yes, she could have seen somebody inject the mare, or she did it herself. In that case she must have known that something was about to happen and wanted her to get out of there”

Jason had been quiet, he took a deep breath and his face was a bit pale. “I must admit that I don’t know diddely-squat about horses but I do know the criminal mind. Anna knew something, I am bloody sure. You don’t kill a person like that just randomly. If she did try to get her mare out of there it meant that she knew that the stables were a target.”

Isadora felt sick again, to the very core. “How did she die?”

Brent was almost sobbing and Thor went over and started rubbing his back. “Easy there chap, let it out”

Isadora knew that Brent had been very fond of Anna and she had in a way been his shield, they had often been seen together and gave the press the impression of being a couple. "Shot through the gut and then set on fire, alive. She probably tried to hide, I had received several phone calls from her but my phone was dead so I didn't answer. "

Jason was pressing his lips together. "We did find what caused the fires"

He pulled a couple of photos out of his coat and Isadora stared at a black and burned box of some sorts, with some wires sticking out of it. It didn't look very threatening at all but Jason placed a finger on the photos with an expression like Churchill declaring war upon Germany. "Insidious and devilish contraptions, made for terror and destruction. If one of these is triggered they cannot be put out and they burn extremely hot. They will set fire to anything, except pure steel. "

Isadora shuddered and felt extremely cold. "They must be hard to come by then?"

Jason shook his head. "Shockingly enough no, if you have money it is easy to get your hands on something like this. You just have to know where to look."

Thor was staring at the photos and his face was very still, without expression. Brent looked as if he had tasted something very foul. "Could the culprit be someone just out there to create fear?"

Jason shrugged. "Hardly, then that person would have targeted people, not animals. No, this is beyond me"

He stared at them. “So I am asking you to help me here, you can be my consultants. The only thing I do know about horses is that they bite in one end and kick in the other and are as easy to steer as a sheet of oil in the open ocean. “

Brent managed to make a sort of a smile. “Of course, we will be glad to help”

Jason took a deep breath of relief. “Good, I am glad. This has to be connected to the industry somehow, horses and sports are big business.”

Thor nodded and he looked as if he was thinking hard. “Yes, it could be that the culprit wants to ruin that?”

Jason made a grimace. “Yes, that is possible and a very believable theory, way better than those who think that this was about insurance fraud. “

Isadora tried to keep her mind clear, to think. “But Anna was a groom, and she was in the stables almost all the time, if she saw something maybe someone else too did notice something out of the ordinary?”

Jason grinned. “I have already taken that into consideration, I have arranged a meeting with all the grooms this very evening, officially to talk about Anna but I want to see if anyone has something to add to the case”

Isadora and Thor suddenly looked like a couple of hound dogs with the scent of their prey right up their nose. “That is clever, the grooms are just there, most don’t even notice them”

Jason looked proud of his own idea. “Yes, so I have good hope there”

Isadora lifted her head. “I want to be there, they know us and I know most of them too, I can tell if somebody is trying to hide something”

Thor nodded firmly, arms crossed over his broad chest. “She does, believe me. Isadora knows everybody in the eventing industry, and most of the people involved in the other equestrian sports too”

Jason smiled. “Good, I don’t know anything like I have previously mentioned, I may make a complete fool of myself if I am to handle this on my own”

Brent grinned. “Yeah, you wouldn’t be able to tell a Clydesdale from a Shetland pony”

Jason tilted his head. “Ah, actually I would, Clydesdales are those humongous beasts with a short tail and lots of hair right? And Shetland ponies are tiny like a dog?”

Brent shook his head. “Well, you are partly right about the Clydesdales but you are thinking about Falabellas, not Shetland ponies. “

Jason frowned. “Partly right?”

Brent nodded solemnly. “Yeah, they aren’t born with short tails, they are cut off”

The investigator shuddered visibly. “What? Why? That sounds awful”

Thor nodded and his eyes were a bit dark. “Most don’t do that these days but there are people who hold onto the tradition. It was done to prevent the tails from getting stuck in the machinery the horses pulled but actually that rarely happens. It is just a thing they did and kept doing”

Jason made an odd gesture, as if to wipe away something bad. “Mankind is truly despicable at times”

Isadora was about to answer when Brent’s phone suddenly rang, the sound was piercing. He answered and they saw that his face fell and he sat down again, very heavily. “Oh God, that is…terrible”

He hid his face in his hands, and the phone fell onto the table, they heard that somebody ended the conversation from the other end. He was obviously distraught and Thor moved over, grasped him by the shoulders. “Brent, what is it?”

The man closed his eyes, there was real pain on his face. “It is Mr Berner, he just had a massive stroke. They don’t think he has much time left. The damage to his brain is too great”

Thor mumbled and Isadora remembered how the man had aged in just a few days. “I was almost waiting for something like that, he was too broken”

Jason looked curious. “The owner of Mr Brewster’s horse right?”

Thor nodded and there was genuine sorrow within the blue eyes . “A grand old man of the horse industry, everybody knew him, and respected him. Many will mourn now”

Isadora stared at Brent. “Ah, what will happen to Crested Moon now? Will you still be allowed to ride her?”

Brent shrugged. “I have no idea, I know that his heir is his granddaughter and she is a bit of a conundrum. She may let me continue using Moon or she’ll cancel the contract, I have no idea”

Thor looked pissed off. “Well, if she does she is a despicable person, only you can ride that mare well, you are used to each other”

Brent took a deep breath. “She has a daughter, sixteen years of age, who thinks she is an expert rider. I fear that…”

His voice broke and Isadora felt so very sorry for him. “She cannot seriously contemplate giving Moon to her kid?! That is insane! The mare is at Olympic level, for how long has her daughter been a rider?”

Brent grunted. “Four years”

Thor snorted, it sounded almost like a horse snorting. “Four years? She can barely compete after four years, let alone ride in high class competitions. That would be a waste of money, Moon is capable of things a horse of those basic levels can barely dream of, and I bet that girl isn’t even all that good right?”

Brent had to grin but his eyes were sad. “She rides like a sack of flour but nobody dares to say that to her”

Isadora shook her head, feeling a bit aspirated. “Damnation, but remember who Moon is Brent, she won’t accept just anybody. If that girl tries to ride her I bet the mare will throw her, like a ragdoll. I have seen how difficult Moon can be at times”

Brent nodded slowly. “Yes, you are right. Moon will never accept it.”

Jason intervened. “If we are to get to that meeting I think we better start to get ready now, the traffic is terrible today.”

Isadora blinked, she still felt a bit weak but her coughing had almost stopped and she was able to walk, although slowly. “I am gonna change, will be back soon”

She returned to her room and Jason sighed and did fidget with his jacket sleeves. “I am glad you are willing to help, the insurance companies are breathing down our necks and my boss is spitting fire as it is already. If it only had been the loss of some horses he wouldn’t have been that strict but two murders? We all feel the pressure”

Thor made a nasty grimace. “I hope he’ll never use that term among us equestrians, just some horses. To us they are family, almost like our children”

Jason smiled. “I have come to understand that yes sir”

Isadora returned, wearing a pair of jeans and a sweater, she tried to look casual and she had braided her hair. With a jacket on she looked as she always had, just some faint redness told that she had been in a fire. They left the room and a huge van was waiting for them outside, the driver was a police officer who smiled and made sure they all got a good seat before he started the van. The fair grounds were closed off still and the grooms were meeting them at another hotel on the other side of the town.

It took some time getting there and Isadora had some time to think as they drove. Thor had placed himself next to her and she had started to realize that he may not have acted this way to just about anybody. But did she dare to believe that he felt something for her, except professional respect and compassion? His behaviour seemed to indicate that yes, he did but could she dare to ask him? No, she was a coward. She could ride a horse down a steep hill at full gallop and still feel naught but excitement but this…it was not anything she was used to.

The grooms were gathered in a small auditorium and Isadora had seen most of them, some came from that other stable which had burned and she saw that a couple were injured but the expressions on their faces told her that they all were willing to help, and that they all mourned the loss of Kenny and Anna. Jason did not hesitate, he walked up to the small podium at the top of the hall and turned around. "We are here to remember Anna Alister but before we start I have a request. We think that Anna may have known what was about to happen, did any of you notice anything out of the ordinary? Did she confide in anyone?"

There was silence, everybody looking at each other, looking confused. Jason sort of moaned and was ready to leave the podium when a thin voice could be heard from the back of the room. A small woman stepped forth, she was very frail looking and pale and she was obviously nervous. Isadora blinked. "Ludmilla?!"

Everybody knew Ludmilla, she wasn't a groom but a person who best could be described as a groupie. A hang around. She was unable to get a real job but stayed at the stables and did small jobs here and there, always eager to do her best but never able to really work well. She was way too fond of her Vodka and her smoke and her health was appalling to say the least. She looked as if a gust of breeze could blow her away at any time. The only thing she was really good at was mucking out stables and brushing floors and so that was what she did most of the time. How she managed to survive was anybody's guess.

Ludmilla and Anna had never been friends, as a matter of fact most would define them as sworn enemies. Anna had hated Ludmilla's alcoholism and felt that it was irresponsible to allow such a person anywhere near the valuable horses. Ludmilla on the other hand had tried to get the job of being Moon's groom even if she was far from qualified and they said that she had tried to bribe her way into the job. Mr Berner had told her to sod off and hated the girl, he was a bit old fashioned and felt that if a woman didn't have a real talent she had nothing to do in a stable. The small frail woman walked up towards them, looking like a frightened little mouse. She held a folder in her arms, it was rather large and filled with papers. "I…Anna came to me, two days before the fire. She just handed me this, and told me not to look at it. But to keep it, and hand it over to the police if something happened. And something did and…"

She lifted the folder and gave it to Brent who frowned. It was heavy and Jason stared at Ludmilla. "She didn't say anything else?"

Ludmilla shook her head, she kept her eyes on the floor and the greasy hair and bad clothes did make her look like a homeless person. “No, I…everybody knew Anna hated me, if it is important…they wouldn’t look for it at my place”

Brent nodded. “Anna was smart. Thank you Ludmilla”

The girl sent them a faint grin and returned to the back of the hall, there was already a man there from the funeral home who was to talk a bit about Anna and Jason grasped Thor and Brent and almost dragged them with him into a different room. Isadora followed, the folder had to be very important. There were some chairs and a table there and Jason switched on the lights and he looked as eager as a horse entering a starting gate. The huge folder contained smaller ones, probably about fifty of them in all and all were neatly marked with numbers and what had to be the year they were referring to.

They were placed in a strict order, the oldest first and Jason stared at them with rather wide eyes. “Guys, I do barely dare to watch this. What if…”

Thor shook his head. “We’ll never know until we check it out. If Anna really was onto something we owe it to her to follow her leads, to the very end. She tried to save Crested Moon so she must have known that something was to go down but she couldn’t have known how or who, then she would have warned us all, I am sure of it. Whatever this is, it must be a theory or an idea, not something she could go to the police with.”

Isadora nodded. “Yes, she must have known a lot, but not all of it.”

Brent took a deep breath, the first folder was also split into three different sections and he opened the first. The investigator held his breath as Brent revealed the first piece of paper within it. It was a page from a newspaper, the headline rather large but the paper was probably a local one. Isadora did leaned over, eager to read what it said. Thor gasped and his eyes were huge and Brent swore so bad it was a miracle the paper didn’t catch fire too. “Two ponies found killed in their stable in Lushdale”

Isadora grasped the article and read it swiftly. “They were found bolted in their boxes, somebody had just killed them. These were kid’s ponies, pets”

Brent went through the rest of the small folder. “Look, more newspaper articles. The ponies were in the news a few times, for having won a competition, and for being comfort animals to the elderly at a local retirement home”

Jason wet his lips. “I think we’ll split the work between us, it will be faster. If all this…”

Thor groaned and pulled his hair back, his eyes were showing his shock. “I know! It is horrific”

Isadora found a pen and a piece of paper in her handbag and sat down with it, she looked very determined. “Alright, you name the year and the number of cases she found, I will try to establish a time line here”

Jason grinned and he looked impressed with her initiative. “Good idea, Anna must have done the same thing”

The men split the folder between them and it soon became clear that Anna had been working hard, she had found cases where horses had been killed over the last seven years, and it had been all over this state and the others around it too. There were even a few cases where donkeys and mules had been murdered and in common was that all the animals had been in the news and been famous either locally or over a larger area. And it was many cases, as many as ten or twelve each year and the worst ones were grotesque. In one case the newspaper articles spoke of three polo ponies who had been found in their paddocks with their left front foot cut off at the fetlock. In another case a herd of protected and genetically rare and endangered mustangs had been chased into a dead end canyon and mowed down with a machine gun. It made Isadora feel faint and the men were pale, Thor looked as if he was about to murder someone.

The work took some hours and when they were done they had a very long list but Isadora saw something important. There were never fewer than eight cases each year and the violence and brutality increased gradually. Jason wiped his forehead. “This is almost like watching a serial killer, they do always evolve over time, what was enough at the beginning will not do it for them at the end”

Brent stared at the list. “We have all sorts of animals here, kid’s ponies, draft horses, steeplechasers, barrel racers and even a bucking bronco from a rodeo. This person must hate the equestrian society"

Isadora wet her lips, she tapped one of the photos with her fingernail, several times. "No, you are wrong. This isn't someone who hates the industry, this is one who hates horses, everything equine! And that hatred is just growing"

Thor raised an eyebrow. "God, you are right, you must be right. This speak of real anger, real hatred."

Jason nodded slowly. "Yes, yes of course"

Brent lifted one of the folders. "But the person isn't a stranger to horses, he knows them and knows how to deal with them, he must have been working with horses"

Thor did turn towards Jason. "At the fairgrounds, was there any sort of surveillance? Cameras?"

Jason sighed. "No, I am sorry. It is too large an area but the guards didn't see anything out of the ordinary"

Isadora did snort. "Yeah right, this person must know exactly how to stay under the radar, to fit inn"

Brent frowned. "Based on what?"

Isadora made a vide gesture. "What we have seen everyday? We know each other, the riders, the grooms…If a spectator does get lost and enters the stable areas he will be seen and escorted out before you can say the word horse. They stick out like a sore thumb!"

Thor was pouting, he was incredibly sexy that way. "You are absolutely right. The person must be someone who knows how to fit in perfectly, to go unnoticed."

Jason did look fascinated. "Someone who does belong?"

Brent nodded. "Yes, most definitely. There were like a hundred thousand spectators at the competitions and only a few of them would have been able to walk around among the stable workers and not be noticed. We horse people do have a certain…I don't know how to describe it but you can see it"

Jason had to laugh. "You are all bow legged?"

Isadora laughed too, it felt good. "Yes, it could be that"

Thor tilted his head. "But back to the serious matters, this person do manage to blend in with the people we do expect to see around us all the time, and at the same time he hates horses?"

Isadora picked up a couple of the news articles, she stared at them with narrow eyes and her brain was working like mad. "Know what? I think I know what his disguise is"

Jason blinked several times, his eyebrows almost touched his hairline. "You do?!"

She nodded. "Look at these articles, two ponies were bolted, some ponies lost their front feet and had to be put down, a draft horse got its throat cut…You cannot just walk up to a horse and take out a pair of bolt cutters and start cutting off their hooves"

Jason frowned. "A veterinarian?"

Isadora shook her head. "Heck no, horses tend to hate the vet, no, I think we all realize who this person do pretend to be?"

Brent and Thor did answer in unison. “A farrier”

Isadora nodded slowly and with some sort of finality, like a business CEO signing an important deal. “Exactly. The horses are used to the farrier, to his tools and his leather apron and scent. They won’t think anything is off it until it is too late”

Jason looked stunned. “That bastard”

Thor nodded and his eyes did shoot blue fire, he was really angry. “Indeed, he is exploiting the fact that all horses have to have their hooves trimmed every now and then and most horses don’t react to it at all. They are so used to it!”

Brent sighed. “And we are used to him too, having somebody walk around in a farriers outfit with a huge box with rasps and thongs and stuff will just look natural, nobody will raise an eyebrow at the sight. We expect to see the farrier there, he is a part of the stage so to speak”

Thor’s voice was dry. “And he can go wherever there are horses and nobody will wonder what he is doing there, goddamn son of a bitch!”

Jason sighed, he looked very tired all of a sudden. “And a huge box is excellent when he wants to hide a fire bomb too”

Isadora stared at the time line she had created. “This is creepy, he started off rather modestly but this last thing? I bet he will go for something even bigger the next time”

Brent took a look at the list. “Yeah, and he won’t wait for very long. He will probably try to outdo himself again”

Thor looked a bit shocked and Jason was scratching his chin. “But this person must spend an awful lot of time just scouring through the newspapers trying to find new victims? It has to take most of the day right?”

Isadora lifted a couple of the newspaper articles. “Most of these are local papers, he either has subscriptions for every little paper there is out there or he uses the internet!”

Brent nodded. “Yeah, you can have a search engine looking for articles concerning horses, even the smallest newspaper these days has a web page.”

Jason clenched his teeth together. “Still, I don’t think this is a person who can hold a normal job, this is a person who is unemployed”

Thor turned his head towards the investigator, he did look puzzled. “Based on what?”

The investigator tilted his head and shrugged. “Look at the different places? He has been all over, and often within a tight time frame too. The attacks have been within a few months of each other, in summer. Then there is nothing again for some months. He is travelling, moving around.”

Isadora wetted her lips. “A travelling salesman? Those are quite common and some do sell horse equipment and such, nobody would find a person like that suspicious if he shows up at a horse owner’s place”

Jason made a grimace. “Maybe, it is a good idea but my gut tells me that this person is too deranged to be able to work. “

Thor sighed. “A person who cannot work, hates horses and travels around all the time. Not a person who is easy to catch”

Isadora yawned, she was getting tired but her adrenaline was high, she wouldn’t be able to sleep even if she tried. “But why hate horses? Maybe that is how we can find him?”

Brent nodded. “Listen to her, she is onto something there”

Jason turned to Isadora. “Okay, why would a person start hating horses, not just a horse but all of them”

Isadora threw a glance at Thor, almost pleadingly. Her throat was dry now and she felt that her head was working a bit slower, she would need a break soon. “Ah, horses can be dangerous? It could be a person who has been injured by a horse and lost the ability to work?”

Jason looked as if he was in some doubt. “Would that be enough to create such a horrible hatred?”

Brent grimaced and cocked his head. “Accidents happen all the time, several people die in horse related accidents each year? It could be somebody who has lost a family member in an accident? A child perhaps?”

Jason nodded. “Now that is more like it, I can understand that. I have seen what that sort of loss can do to a person”

Isadora took a deep breath. “Yeah, it can make a person snap. And if that person is a bit frail from before….”

Thor nodded eagerly, his hair did look like a mane around his face. “He loses a kid, loses a job or more, loses his very existence and wants revenge…I think we are going somewhere here”

Jason smiled. "Yes! I am so glad I have you here"

He made some notes. "But still, we haven't come any closer to finding out who this is"

Brent pointed at the folder. "Anna must have seen the timeline too and realized that the show was a possible target, and she also knew that there were too much money involved for anybody to listen to her if she just came forth and claimed that somebody would want to kill the horses. "

Isadora stared at the list. "He may strike again, very soon"

Jason looked a bit nervous. "Really? Where?"

Thor snapped his fingers, his eyes were a bit distant. "Somewhere with many horses, famous ones. And not too far from here"

Isadora and Brent spoke at the same time and it didn't sound like anything anybody could understand so he closed his mouth and allowed her to speak alone. "The Wettersfield race track, it is opening for the season tomorrow and there are a lot of very famous racers gathering there now"

Jason raised an eyebrow. "Holy fuck, of course. And it is all over the news. I have got to make a call!"

He left the room swiftly and Brent stared at Isadora. "You are pale, and sweating. Are you alright?"

Thor made huge eyes and sat down next to her. "Oh I am so sorry, I didn't think…you need some rest, and food!"

Isadora felt a bit embarrassed. She didn't want to slow them down, lives could be at stake now. There were a lot of people working at those racing stables and they would do everything to protect their horses. “I am alright, really”

Thor placed a hand on her forehead. “No, you are not! We need to get some food into you, soon!”

Brent nodded sternly. “Yes, but first, we need to find that goddamn bastard and do it soon. I wonder if there were any of those cases where there were surveillance videos? Some of the animals belonged to rich owners, and they were expensive too?”

Isadora lifted one of the folders with some hope. “The two yearling Clydesdales which got poisoned at the Budweiser breeding farm?”

Thor shook his head. “They have surveillance in the stables yes, but not out in the fields. And the horses were murdered in the pasture with strychnine laced oats. No, I think I saw a familiar name here somewhere though…”

He went over the folders with great speed and held up one. “Here, I know this lady”

Isadora read the headline. “Three of Mrs Ekdahl’s best brood mares killed by poisonous hay?”

Brent frowned. “Isn’t that the old…ah…eccentric widow of trainer Ekdahl?”

Isadora stared at Brent. “The old what?”

Brent blushed deeply. “Uh…well, she has a certain…reputation”

Thor laughed out loud and there was genuine mirth within his gaze. “She is well known as a bit of a dragon, and a cougar to boot.

She loves pretty men and she runs her stables with an iron fist. Excellent breeder and a person who has forgotten more about thoroughbreds than most people will ever learn but she can be a bit of a bitch at times and very straight forward, and not in a nice way. If she doesn't like someone she will let you know, there and then"

Isadora shuddered and hissed. "A dragon, right. But you think she may have had surveillance videos?"

Thor nodded. "I'll ask Jason when he does return"

Brent frowned and there was a hint of a smirk within his eyes "Don't tell me she has made a move on you?"

Thor turned red like a beet. "Ah, actually…"

Brent snickered and his eyes were glittering with boyish charm. "Oh she did didn't she? That old…bat!"

Thor managed to look dignified again. "I was way younger then, and I was there representing my father, to buy a colt of her. But she backed off when I said I wasn't interested. She was…in her late sixties I think?"

Isadora laughed. "That must have been precious to see"

Jason entered the room again, waving his phone. "I have made some calls, they will increase the security, they don't want a repetition of what happened here but I don't think they are taking it very seriously. They ought to remove all the horses from the stables."

Brent sighed, "And send them where? There are huge amounts of money involved Mr Armaggio, billions. The races have to be run or people will lose a lot of wealth and to some that is way more important the possible death of some race horses and grooms. "

Jason looked a bit shocked. "I cannot understand this…"

Thor nodded. "Yeah, but the owners are filthy rich in most cases Mr Armaggio and to them money are what life is about. They just go on, wearing blinkers and thinking it won't happen to them. Ignoring danger is a part of everyday life to them. If they were careful they wouldn't breed horses which are bound to break down sooner or later or spend hundreds of thousands on genetic testing and new training methods which may or may not work"

Jason frowned and his eyes revealed his disbelief. "Bound to break down? That doesn't sound good at all"

Brent nodded sternly. "The thoroughbred industry isn't good, believe me. A horse shouldn't be broken as a yearling and ridden hard in races before his bones have had time to set properly. And yet they do. They are supposedly faster when they are young. And bloodlines which create fast horses are overused, even when they also breed for brittle bones"

Thor nodded. "Speed is everything! If they can win a few times with an animal it is worth it, even if they have to shoot it afterwards"

Jason shook his head. Thor held up the newspaper article about Mrs Ekdahl. "Did this woman have cameras? I know her, we may get help there"

Jason frowned and stared at the article. “It happened in…Riverrest? That is four counties to the west of here? I can see if I can get in contact with the police there.”

He lifted his phone. “God bless the smart phone, I remember before, when we had to drag around on phones the size of a suitcase, heavy as fuck”

He left the room again and Thor took his own phone and walked into a corner. They heard that he called somebody and his voice changed a lot, became smooth and gentle, very convincing. He turned around and smiled. “I have the old bat’s phone number, I remembered the name of her trainer and she remembered me”

Jason returned, grinning from one ear to the next. “Yes, there were videos, and they caught something. But the old…b…the widow does still have them.”

Brent grinned. “Right, so we will have to go there. Can you tame a shrew Thor?”

The tall blonde grinned and winked. “I am certain I can yes, and we must get there asap. Now let me see if my charm is forgotten or not”

He made a call and they heard different voices, he did explain the reason he was calling and they heard a very loud and shrill woman’s voice which did sound rather upset but it was very obvious that they were welcome, more than welcome, and that she was very eager to help them. Thor ended the call and shook his head, his eyes were huge. “I first reached her personal assistant. The old she wolf is getting senile, but she does remember everything regarding her horses, even though the brain is a wee bit out of practice one may say"

Jason nodded. "So, we are going?"

Thor grinned. "We are going, and we will stop on the way and get some food and rest. Isadora does need it."

She tried to smile. "I have to call the nurse, I think I can handle it on my own now. I just need to bring the inhaler and the other stuff from the hotel"

Thor nodded and his eyes were soft now. "I will help you with that, we need to work fast now, very fast. "

Half an hour later they were on their way and the hotel staff had packed their stuff for them so it was ready when they arrived. Thor checked out and Brent managed to get one of the best grooms to take care of Moon while he was away. Jason had managed to get hold of a mini bus and the seats could be flipped down so one could sleep, it was a very smart move for they were tired. On the way out of the city they stopped by a restaurant and Thor bought them all a mammoth meal which made Isadora feel like a stuffed animal. She barely managed to get back into the minibus before she fell asleep, like a log. Thor placed a blanket over her and smoothed out her hair, a sort of gentle light in his eyes.

Brent was whispering to him. "You are a bit taken by her aren't you?"

Thor sat down and put on his seat belt. "Yeah, I have been for a long time too. But she has always been so busy and you know, they call her the ice princess and it isn't for nothing. She works way too hard for her own good"

Brent snickered. "You have got to come clean with her, I bet she is just as taken by you, just not able to believe that you are interested"

Thor frowned. "You think so?"

Brent nodded and smiled wryly. "Yeah, I am actually one hundred percent certain. I may be gay man, but I have eyes. And attraction is attraction after all. Gender is irrelevant here"

Thor blushed and looked a bit embarrassed. "Right…I may…"

Brent waved a finger. "No may Thor, you are gonna confess to her before this mess is over, you hear? She deserves it and so do you"

Thor just blushed even deeper and didn't answer.

It was getting dark now and the bus was hitting the main road, there was a lot of traffic and the driver was obviously a skilled one for he managed to keep a very even speed even when there were whole lanes blocked by slow moving vehicles.

Jason was half asleep, Isadora was asleep and so was Thor and Brent was dozing in his seat, he was about to drift into real sleep when his phone buzzed. It was the groom who was taking care of Moon and for a moment he froze, fearing that something was wrong with the mare. Then he saw it was a text message. "Turn on the news, channel three, NOW!"

He held his breath and opened the browser of his phone, found the channel and what he saw made him gasp and feel light headed and almost like jelly all over. "Oh no, we were too late"

He gathered his thoughts and shook Jason, not too gently. The investigator blinked and coughed and stared at Brent. "Are we there already?"

Brent shook his head. "No, take a look at this"

He held his phone out and Jason sat up so fast the seat was creaking, his eyes got huge and you could count his molars. "Oh…fuck! God no!"

The images on the screen were hellish to say the least, if the fire of the stables of the fairgrounds had been bad this was on a whole new level, it looked like an inferno, like images from the great forest fires which had ravaged whole cities out west.

Jason was trembling. "How?"

Brent opened more tabs. "Here, somebody did fly a small crop duster over the entire area, sprayed it all with what they only describe as a sort of napalm. It was like a bomb went off, everywhere at once"

Jason moaned and looked over at Thor and Isadora. "I have to wake them up…"

Brent grasped him by the sleeve. "NO, don't you dare. They need to sleep and Isadora doesn't need to see this, she'll collapse."

Jason closed his eyes, there was pain on his face. "Right, you are of course right. But I need to make calls, there has to have been human lives lost"

Brent tried to smile, but he couldn't "Do that, I will make sure that the two get their rest"

Jason went up to the front and he almost whispered and when he returned he was very pale. "Six people are confirmed dead but another ten are missing. And they fear that at least a hundred horses are dead too, they did manage to get five out of there alive, just five!"

Brent groaned and closed his eyes, he was getting a headache. "Dosing the entire area with napalm, that is devious. Stables are dusty and there are plenty of flame able materials there. Goddamn it, this is one real creep"

Jason nodded. "Indeed"

Brent sighed. "There is nothing we can do about that now, we just have to do whatever we can to catch the devil, we will be there in two hours. Try to rest. We need our minds to be calm now, more than ever"

Jason made a croaking sound, like a frog that was choking. "As if I ever will be able to rest after that…"

Brent made an ugly grimace and patted him on the shoulder. "You will, just focus on the job ahead"

The two remained awake until they reached the huge estate where Mrs Ekdahl lived, it was immense and it was very obvious that this was the home of a very fat bank account. One which was larger than the budget of a small country. It did look like a mansion from the seventeen hundreds and not a leaf or straw of grass was out of order, the morning light was still some hours away but the place was lit up like a fourth of July parade.

Brent took a deep breath and he didn't want to do this but he had to. He shook Thor gently. "Thran? Wake up, we are there"

The blonde opened his eyes and yawned. "Already? I feel as if I have slept just an hour"

Brent managed to smile. "But it has been at least four, ah, there has been an incident, again!"

Thor tensed up, the eyes got sharp as lances. "It is bad isn't it?"

Jason swallowed hard. "It is…gruesome. The racetrack…all the stables…"

Thor heaved for air, his eyes were wild. "Oh no, goddamn it!"

Brent sighed. "That is just the start of it yeah"

Thor turned around. "Let me wake Isadora, she needs this delivered to her gently"

They were driving up to the main building now and he did take her hand, hating himself for having to do this to her but there were no way around it. "Isa? Do you hear me?"

Isadora had been dreaming again, a pleasant dream this time, about riding over the pastures back home on one of her horses and she grunted as she was ripped away from it. She opened her eyes and saw the lights outside and felt that the car was parked. "Oh, we are there?"

Thor smiled but his eyes were showing that not everything was well. "Yes, we have arrived. Isadora, I am so sorry but.."

She saw their expressions and her eyes got huge, she grasped onto Thor's hand so hard they heard bones creaking. "No?!!"

He nodded and looked down. "I am afraid so, the shithead did hit the racetrack, it is very bad"

She grasped for her phone but Thor snatched it from her. "You do not need to see it, it is a fire, again. And you don't want PTSD, it is enough that Brent and I probably will suffer from it for life after this"

She did grind her teeth together. "Right, but we are to speak with that widow now aren't we? And hopefully see if we can find that…piece of filth"

Thor nodded and he touched her hair gently. "Yes we are, shape up folks, the lady of the house is all about class"

Isadora brushed her hair and fixed her make up and the men straightened their jackets and made sure that it wasn't visible that they had slept in a car. They were met by the lady's butler, a man who would look just right in an episode of Poirot and he was obviously distraught. "I must ask you gentlemen to be careful, one of the lady's horses was killed in that ghastly fire tonight, she is…fragile"

Thor nodded and walked in front of them, they entered a huge library which was filled with images of horses, Isadora recognized some of them as famous racehorses through history. A massive painting of a large red stallion did take up the main part of the wall and she was rather sure it had to be the famous Secretariat. The horse had been able to outrun just about anything on four legs and it wasn't until it was put down due to acute laminitis that they discovered it was because he had a heart which was abnormally large, completely healthy just four times the normal size. It was if you took the engine out of an ordinary sports car and replaced it with one from a formula one racer.

The woman sitting in a chair did look like a wraith, normally she was probably the very image of elegance and dignified grace but now she was just heartbroken. She had been crying and she wore a nightgown and a coat and her hair was unkempt and thin. She wrung her hands and Thor walked over and bent over, gave her a swift hug. The woman sobbed and her eyes were confused and glassy. "Oh Mr Oswold, they killed my beautiful Spring rose!"

Thor nodded, his voice was soft and gentle, as if he was speaking to a child. "I know my dear, I know. But we are here to catch the one who did this, and killed your brood mares"

The woman's eyes were distant. "We had such hopes for those foals, the dams were descendants of the great Secretariat and the sires were among the very best, European blood you see. "

Thor stroked the thin grey hair, there was genuine compassion within his face and Isadora felt her heart melt completely. "I know, they would have been magnificent, the very best"

She sobbed again and it was obvious that her mind was rather clouded. "They said that we had fed them mouldy hay?! But that is impossible, I check the feed myself, and the investigation showed that they had been fed poison hemlock. The insurance company…oh I hate those pricks"

Brent had to smile. “No don’t we all”

The butler was standing there, discrete and he bowed slightly. “I have prepared the surveillance video you asked for gentlemen, ma’am”

There was a TV set at the back of the room and the butler turned it on, the picture was a bit grainy but they could see alright. A white van without licence plates stopped outside of the gates, and a man exited, he wore a sort of dark suit and Brent blinked in disbelief. “Ah what?!”

Jason leaned inn closer. “A wet suit?”

The butler nodded with his nose up. “The previous day we had a problem with the water supply, one of the main pipes got clogged and the plumbers had to send a diver down into the reservoir to unclog the intake valve. It was a huge piece of tarpaulin which had gotten stuck”

Thor looked as if he had bitten into something incredibly sour “More like placed there I bet. This one does research his targets, and does it very thoroughly. If someone saw him he would just say that he had forgotten something by the reservoir and needed to retrieve it”

The butler raised an eyebrow, he reminded Isadora of a parrot her aunt had owned once, it too used to raise its eyebrows when it was shocked. “Dear me, oh my, such a scoundrel”

He whispered to them. “The lady used some language I will prefer not to repeat but it was…salty. But the diver wore his mask the entire time so we would not been able to tell that it wasn't him no"

Thor nodded and his expression was cold. "I bet."

The video changed, the man in the wet suit climbed the wall and slid down and disappeared. Then the view changed again, now they saw a man wearing a pair of stable overalls and wellingtons walking casually over the yard towards the stables but he wore a huge hat and he was limping. "That is a fake limp if I ever have seen one"

Brent's voice was dry and Jason nodded. "Yeah. But we cannot see his face goddamn it. Not even once. He knows where the cameras are aimed."

The man disappeared out of sight and the video showed that about five minutes passed by before he returned, he had carried a small white bag in his hand and now it was gone. The butler grunted. "We found the plastic bag in the manure pile the day after, no finger prints of course"

Mrs Ekdahl wailed and her arms were flailing around, she looked absolutely confused. "My beautiful Rose, she was my best filly, oh what am I to do now?"

The video showed that the man disappeared and then he climbed back over the wall, minus the overalls. The van disappeared shortly after that.

The butler stopped the video. "The van used standard tires, there weren't any traces anywhere. The piece of canine excrement was thorough"

Isadora frowned. “The mares were poisoned with hemlock?”

The butler nodded, his voice low. “Yes, a very nasty sub species which grows in this area of the state. It is lethal to horses”

Brent closed his eyes. “The man does indeed know horses.”

Isadora did almost growl. “And what’s more, he knows about dangerous herbs. He isn’t some stupid redneck this one, he has knowledge and he is able to plan ahead and do it well”

Jason swallowed, his Adams apple was moving up and down. “Then he isn’t really mad is he? He has to be sane, but evil”

Thor made a grimace and shrugged. “I think he can be as mad as a hatter and yet in some ways still very smart, but he has to make a mistake sooner or later”

Jason stared, his eyes were huge. “Later, goddamn it man, there can be no later! The man is a murderer, not only of equines. What’s next? A bomb at a 4H fair? We cannot wait, we have to get him!”

Isadora nodded. “Yes, we must catch him, like yesterday! If he escalates the way he has lately the next attack will be in a few days”

Brent rubbed the bridge of his nose. “Yeah, you are right. But we didn’t see anything of importance on that video.”

Jason made a grimace. “Oh but we did. He knew about the cameras but he forgot one very important thing”

They stared at him. “What?”

Jason smiled. “What an experienced eye can see. I have seen countless such videos, run it again, I am sure I can find something to focus on”

The butler nodded obediently and started the video and Jason was staring at it with narrow eyes, he was deeply concentrated. “Right, stop”

The butler stopped the video. “What do you see?”

Jason pointed at the screen. “Right here, as he climbs the wall, do you see? He is not using his right arm that much as his left?”

Isadora nodded. “Yes, he could be left handed?”

Jason went all the way up the screen, his face was that of a hungry wolf with the scent of a wounded deer in his nose. “No, look at the suit and the glove which covers his right arm and hand? It looks odd…move the video a few seconds…thanks”

The picture moved a few frames and they stared. “Ah, right. See?”

Thor squinted. “There is something odd about his elbow?”

Jason knocked a finger against the screen. “He is an amputee. He has lost his lower right arm”

Isadora gasped and the widow in the chair squealed, she was listening and obviously trying to understand it all. “Damn it, you are right, the arm is too rigid.”

Jason smiled. “Yes, I think we are to change our idea of this being someone who has lost a family member, this is somebody who has been injured by a horse, the initial idea!”

Brent made a sort of groan. “Not necessarily no, it could be that the lost limb is just a coincidence. But whatever the cause, the person is clearly very sick”

Jason was about to answer when a door flew open at the other end of the room and a man wearing a uniform entered, he bowed and they could see that he was a bit pale and the eyes were huge. “Sirs, the silent alarm, it has been triggered!”

The butler jerked, as if somebody had put a red hot poker to his nether regions. “What!! Where man, where?!”

The servant swallowed and his eyes were bulging slightly. “The upper stable sir, two minutes ago.”

Jason swore like a sailor and Mrs Ekdahl let out a piercing wail. “My darlings, he is gonna kill my darlings!”

The butler spun around like a top. “We installed silent alarms and motion detectors in all the stables after the incident, all very well hidden. This cannot be some bug in the system”

Jason shook himself out of the shock. “Call the local police and tell them to come fast but quietly. Do you have weapons here?”

The butler did grin, a nasty smile. “Better, we have our security expert, Lothar”

The door flew open again and a behemoth of a man ran into the room, he wore a sort of army uniform and he was packing heat, to say the least. He carried an Ar 15 and had a huge colt in his belt and he was obviously very eager. Mrs Ekdahl sobbed desperately. “Please, save them”

Lothar stared at the small crowd. “Is this the bastard who killed those mares? In that case allow me to skin him before the police arrives”

The man had a German accent thicker than pea soup and some scars, he looked as if he was picked out of some old war movie where he had played the role of a nasty Nazi officer. Jason nodded. “Granted, do you have a handgun, I don’t carry usually”

The huge man handed Jason a Beretta and Mrs Ekdahl was sobbing again, wringing her hands. She looked terrified. “Hurry hurry, save them”

Lothar turned around. “Follow me, the stable is not far from here. Mrs Ekdahl keeps the young fillies there”

They ran and when they entered the yard behind the house they saw that Lothar wasn’t the only person alerted. There were at least five people there, wearing SWAT equipment and carrying huge guns. Thor ran behind the huge soldier, it was obvious that the man was a mercenary and so were his co-workers. It was quite clear that the old lady did have money enough to employ her own little army. The stable was dark, it was very quiet there and Brent and Isadora walked behind Thor and Lothar, the others spread out quietly and without a sound, they were sneaking forth and Isadora held her breath.

If this was the same person he would have had to travel very fast but if he had a plane it was possible. Lothar held a small screen and he whispered. “We have one person, who entered through the door. He is still inn there.”

Jason whispered back. “Do not kill the suspect, I need to…interrogate him”

The stable door was ajar, and it was rather quiet in there. Isadora saw that the boxes were dark, the horses were probably sleeping but the lights had been turned on in one of them and they did hear motions. The small group was sneaking forth, staying low and it was amazing to see that a man as huge as Lothar was able to move like that, without a sound. The stable was tidy and there wasn’t a speckle of dust anywhere, the horses didn’t react at all to the presence and it told Isadora that these were well taken care off. They would trust humans and didn’t anticipate anything bad. Jason and Lothar moved forth, the others were signalled to stay back and they took refuge in an open box, just in case. They would try to avoid firing guns in there, it could most definitely spook the nervous animals.

Lothar crawled along, stopped in front of the boxdoor. They heard a voice which was whispering and a horse was obviously standing there in the box, a grey mare which looked a bit confused. The ears were clipping back and forth and she snorted. Jason held his gun ready and Lothar grasped the box door. These were the type of doors which can be slid to the side completely and the man was strong. He pushed the door all the way to the side in just one go and they all saw. A small man stood there with some sort of harness and he had a step ladder standing there behind the filly, his pants were already on his knees and his boxer shorts were tented. He was blinking, like a deer caught in the headlights and Lothar let out a roar worthy of a lion and jumped into the box, grasping for the tiny man. “You fucking pervert!”

The man squealed like a school girl and ran, he was surprisingly fast, like a squirrel and he raced out through the open box door with a speed which was impressive since he was trying to pull his pants up while moving. He wore thick glasses and was more than a wee bit on the fluffy side but the legs moved like drumsticks and he was in the way towards the exit when Isadora jumped out of the box she had been hiding inn and kicked the man right in the crotch with both gusto and power. The guy collapsed, grasping his crotch with both hands, eyes bulging as if he was some deep water fish which had been pulled to the surface way too fast. “Eeeeeep”

Jason was on the run too, he grasped the man and held him and Lothar had the harness in his hands and used it to tie the guy up like a ham. Thor stared, his eyes were shooting lightening and Jason stared at the harness. “What the heck is that?”

Thor looked as if he wanted to kick the guy too. “A harness used during coverings, to prevent the mare from kicking the stallion if she has a sudden change of heart.”

Jason looked as if he had seen the light all of a sudden. “Ah….aaaalright, get up you fucking idiot, trying to be the big stud are you? Not anymore, Isadora her is a rider, she has impressive leg muscles for sure”

The man panted, face red and eyes still bulging and Lothar holsteredhis handgun. “Right, I better tell the lady that this isn’t a case of somebody trying to kill her fillies, just some nut brain trying to fuck one of them"

Thor nodded. "Do that, but tell me, how come you work for Mrs Ekdahl? You are an army guy right?"

The huge man shrugged. "The old lady is a bit nuts, and at times a complete fruitcake but she is fair, and honest. And she pays me well too, what's not to like about that? And I do love horses"

Thor bowed his head and Lothar and the other men grasped the man and hauled him off. In the distance they saw the lights from several police cruisers. The culprit would most certainly be arrested and thrown into jail so fast it would make a jet look slow. Isadora was a bit dark eyed and her face was showing that she didn't like this situation at all. Thor walked over and hugged her. "You kick like a mule my friend"

Isadora hissed. "Yeah, as if he didn't deserve it? I have come across those creeps before, before long animals won't be enough and then a kid is his next victim"

Thor sighed but his eyes were filled with admiration "I thought so, but you stopped him. Very well done"

Brent closed the box door and threw some hay into the box, the mare looked rather calm, she had no idea she was saved from being violated by a human just in the nick of time. The culprit was being processed by the police and it was rather obvious that they were using gauntlets instead of silk gloves. Mrs Ekdahl probably sponsored them with money each year, the zeal with which the guy was cuffed and stuffed into the cruiser was impressive. Jason was quiet and he held his phone, as if he was half expecting more bad news each second. “We still need to find that bastard who torched those stables, he is out there folks”

Isadora took a deep breath. “I did notice something about those articles?”

The men turned towards her. “Yeah?”

Isadora blushed slightly, she felt oddly self-conscious. “The owners were barely mentioned. I mean, there were probably a lot of articles in those papers regarding horses but I bet that those saw the owners as the important part and the animals were just mentioned.”

Thor nodded. “You are right, he goes for cases where the animals have centre stage so to speak.”

She made a swift grimace, as if she was tasting something bad. “Uh, we need to check the papers, all of them. There has to be a clue there, we need to find every article which speaks about a horse or horses and don’t mention people that much”

Jason snapped his fingers. “Excellent idea, I can get someone to start looking right away”

Thor did shake his head. “No, it won’t do. He has probably already chosen a target, but I think I have an idea”

Brent frowned. “Ah, you are mad now? I hope you know that?”

Jason did look confused. “What are you referring to?”

Thor did take a deep breath. “We can create a bait article, drawing him inn. We can make something which will make him forget about whatever target he is focusing on now and force him to act"

Isadora gaped. "That is smart, no, genius. But what sort of article?

Thor made a thin grin, his face was suddenly a bit sinister. "I do happen to know a reporter who is willing to do whatever it takes for me, and I have a lot of pictures. Beside, my ranch is in the middle of nowhere, and I have contacts."

Jason opened and closed his mouth like a book, then he blinked and coughed. "That is truly insane, you are endangering your own property, your own horses"

Thor squinted, he did look sinister. "Am I now? Like I said, I have contacts, and the place is easy to protect. I will of course be taking my own precautions and if he doesn't know that we expect him, well, we can create one hell of a surprise party"

Jason looked a bit shocked. "That may actually work! Crazy as it is. But it has to be done fast. Who knows where he is determined to strike next"

Brent had been using his phone, he was working fast and he held it up. "Here, this is where he'll strike, if we cannot stop him"

They watched the screen. Isadora moaned loudly and turned her head away and Thor stared at Jason, his eyes were both hard and pleading at the same time. "See? There will be at least ten thousand spectators to those competitions, the world championships of marathon driving is a huge event"

Jason gulped, his eyes were huge. “Oh God, and they start in less than a week? How are we to stop them? The area needs to be evacuated, what if he use that plane tactics again?”

Isadora raised an eyebrow. “Easy, pretend to be a terrorist, call inn a bomb threat.”

Jason just gaped. “I am a cop goddamn it, I cannot just…”

Lothar had been listening to them after the cops took off and he grinned viciously. “But I can, I sound like a terrorist right? I can pretend to be of some unknown obscure group. I can make sure that they remove both people and horses from the area”

Isadora stared at him in surprise. “How?”

Lothar tilted his head and the man was indeed terrifying. “Anthrax, I know somebody who does know somebody, if they receive a wee bit of that stuff, as a demonstration only, they are forced to take it seriously right?”

Isadora almost choked. “Are you nuts? That is really lethal”

Lothar just shrugged and Jason grunted. “There has to be another way, we can call them and tell them the truth? They have seen what happened at the race track?”

Isadora crossed her arms over her chest. “And warn the bastard that somebody is onto him? If they suddenly cancel he’ll know for sure. But if they have to evacuate all of a sudden it seems way more real, this sort of shit happens quite often these days”

Thor nodded. “Yeah, and some of the people competing there is from countries which are a bit dubious to say the least, make it sound as if this is a protest against the presence of say…Saudi Arabians? They have pissed off many people over the years"

Lothar did snicker. "Of course, I can come up with a great name for the group, but it has to happen tonight"

Isadora did stare at the men. "Well what are you waiting for? Thor, make the calls to that reporter, and Jason, warn the police that the threat is a fake but tell them to act as if it is real. We have to get moving, now!"

Jason took a deep deep sigh, his eyes were dark. "Right, fine. Go ahead, make the call but make it good. And Thor, make sure that you are barely mentioned in the article but that the name of the ranch is given several times"

Thor grinned and showed thumbs up, then he ran off and so did Lothar, Isadora could only keep her fingers crossed. This had to work.

Thor did return after fifteen minutes, he was grinning. "An article is being published tomorrow, with the names of some of my horses and lots of pictures and lots of bragging too. And I was barely even mentioned. If he cannot attack that driving competition my ranch will be a perfect substitute"

Jason rolled his eyes. "And I pray to God that you do have the resources to prepare for this?"

Thor just smiled enigmatically. "Of course I do. Do not worry."

Isadora frowned. "But we need to get there right? And that takes days?"

Thor shook his head. “Nope, there is an airfield not far from the ranch, and I have a deal with a small air company, we can fly over in a couple of hours, no big deal”

Brent looked as if he had his doubts. “The culprit used a plane, if he does that again?”

Thor smiled. “I expect him to fly inn, to drive takes days. But I know the guys at the tower and they will keep an eye on all air traffic. After 9/11 all planes must have a identification beacon and if one plane does show up on the radar and doesn’t have one? Well, he’ll get an F-18 up his arse very fast”

Isadora nodded. “Yes, so you will be warned?”

Thor nodded slowly. ”Exactly, even if the culprit does land somewhere else the tower will see him and notify me. The people out in the wilderness do help each other, we have to.”

Jason swallowed again and he did look a bit nervous. “Do we need reinforcements?”

Thor shook his head. “I have called for the cavalry already. I just need to make one call and a jet is ready at the runway for us”

Brent chuckled. “You are acting like an ordinary cowboy all the time, but in truth you are richer than the bank. I just cannot figure you out Thor”

The tall blonde did shrug. “It is a defence, believe me. Growing up being the son of a multi millionaire and still having to wear boots and jeans to school each day wasn’t easy but it did toughen me up”

Isadora hadn’t known that about him “Really?”

He nodded. “Dad was very adamant that I had to learn from the bottom up, not from the top and down. He didn’t want me to become an arrogant asshole”

Isadora blushed, “I must say that he did succeed, rather well”

Jason clapped his hands. “Right, then shall we? The airport is an hour away after all”

They saw that the butler was approaching them, he did bow at the waist. “The lady is very grateful for your help and she will make sure that you arrive at the airport in style. The idiot who tried to…have his wicked way…with her filly will probably never see the light of day again, the lady knows the shrinks and they will make sure that the sentence is a long one”

Isadora almost snickered, the old fashioned style the butler spoke in made it sound comical even though it wasn’t. “That is very good thank you, thank the lady for her generosity and tell her that I will give her a call the moment the bastard is caught”

Thor smiled at the butler who bowed again. “Of course sir, the limousine is waiting”

Brent had to grin. “A limousine, I can count the times I have ridden in one on one hand”

Isadora giggled. “I have never been in one before, I wonder if it has food? I am getting hungry again”

Thor patted her on the back. “I think we are guaranteed a very pleasant drive to the airport”

The limo was a huge one, the length of a bus and Isadora was thrilled to see that there indeed was food waiting for them, several pizzas all freshly baked. It was odd, normally she would be in bed at this time of the day, but now she was wide awake. The limo also had very comfortable seats, and enough booze to make an army dead drunk. The butler had called the airport and a plane would be ready for them, the lady had organized that too.

Isadora ate enough pizza to yet again feel stuffed and Thor was busy making calls. Brent was also on the phone and Jason was mailing his bosses and explaining everything. The drive took a while, and Isadora began to feel drowsy and Thor found a pillow and a warm blanket. She fell asleep and slept like a log until they reached the airport. The plane was already on the runway, it was a small private jet and Isadora had never flown in one before. It was very luxurious and filled with all sorts of food and drink but she found a bed and crashed onto it as soon as they were airborne. She was simply too tired to care much now.

Thor did wake her up when they were on final approach to the small airport where they were to land. It was a very small one, this jet was about the ideal size to land there but larger planes couldn't get back up again, the runway was too small. Thor told them that there had been a large plane taking off though, once. An army C-130 which had been sent there to pick up the remains of an army plane which had crashed in the mountains and they had used Jato rockets to make the huge bird take off from the short runway. It had been quite a spectacle. The tower was rather tall and very modern, and there was a high and solid fence around the entire area. It wasn't to keep people out, it was to keep animals away from the runway. If a plane hit a deer or even worse, a moose during landing or take off it would be a disaster. There was a huge truck waiting for them, Thor walked over and the driver was a stocky man in his late fifties with a long pony tail and a scarred face. Isadora was rather sure that he was a native. Thor grinned. "This is Joe, he is the one in charge of the ranch when I am not at home."

Joe nodded slowly and looked as if he already knew everything which was worth knowing about them from the first glance, he didn't seem like the kind of man who spends too much time speaking at all. "I have made the calls boss, they'll be here tomorrow"

Thor just smiled. "Good, now, let us get going. We all need some rest and a bath and then we need to plan ahead"

The truck had an odd engine sound and Brent frowned. "That is not an original motor is it?"

Thor shook his head. "No, one of my workers is a bit of a wizard when it comes to cars, he did replace the engine of this one with one from a Mack truck. "

Isadora just rolled her eyes, men and machines! The ranch was more than an hour of driving from the air strip and the landscape which was visible now underneath a gorgeous sunrise was amazing, it was wild and ragged and there were holts of trees and meadows and cliffs. It looked like paradise and Isadora saw that there were fences and pastures as they got closer to the main buildings. The ranch itself was placed between two rather steep cliffs and it did look like it had been born out of the ground with gorgeous notched timber buildings and soft earthly colours. A rather large holt of trees was growing to the east of it and Thor did step out of the car and smiled. “Welcome to Greenvale, now, let’s find you a place to rest”

Isadora was impressed, this place did look very old fashioned but she saw that it was rather modern still, the main house larger than many mansions she had seen and way more cosy. There was a couple of men meeting them, one smelled of horse and had to be the stable manager and another one looked like a cowboy from a movie, he was walking with a limp and his clothes looked as if they had been dragged through a tornado at least twice. “Boss, I have prepared the stable.”

Thor smiled. “Good Juan, and the fences are checked yeah?”

The cowboy grunted. “Yes, the sensors are in place and working”

Brent frowned. “Sensors?”

Thor smiled, a sly smile. “Motion sensors, and cameras. All very well hidden”

He walked through the hall and they entered a sort of side wing. There were several rooms there and Isadora and Brent were given one each as was Jason too. The rooms were large and airy and very nice and Isadora found that she in fact was sleepy still. But first there was a meal being served and they found that the place had many people working for Thor, there were at least four people employed there who took care of the buildings and then there were horse trainers and grooms and other farm workers too. Apparently the ranch did also have some cattle and a building with large pigs. Everybody would eat together and since it was early still many were there for breakfast or an early lunch. Thor presented Isadora and Brent and Jason to the crowd and everybody listened very attentive when Thor explained the situation.

Isadora managed take a quick shower after the meal, then she hit the bed and slept very well for some hours before she was awakened by an elderly native woman with a gentle smile and very soft eyes. Clean clothes were waiting for her and she got up and brushed her hair and prepared for the day. She had no idea of what it would bring.

She entered a large living room with a huge TV and the men were already seated, Jason was on the phone but Thor saw her and he smiled widely, gestured for her to join them. "Look, here is the article. It is brilliant"

Isadora grasped the Ipad Thor handed her and she frowned. The headline was very bold. "Heir to the throne" it said and there was an image of a very large grey horse. It looked a bit like Silver Ghost but was darker in colour and it looked a bit feisty. Thor grinned again, from one ear to the other. "That is General Flint, he is a half brother to Silver Ghost and a handful but I made the reporter write that I will use him from now on. I told him to really brag about the horse"

Isadora blinked. "Is he any good?"

Thor shook his head. “No, he cannot be used for eventing yet. Too hot headed, I can ride cross country with him but he won’t do in a dressage contest at all. But nobody needs to know that. I do have another horse I think about using from now on, maybe.”

Brent tilted his head. “Still, he is just as good looking as Silver was”

Thor made a grimace but nodded. “Yes, but he is stockier though, heavier.”

Isadora swallowed. “Are you sure that the suspect will see that article?”

Thor nodded and sat down next to her. “Yes, the reporter made sure to add all the possible words the bastard must be searching for, and the driving championship was cancelled just an hour ago. It was all over the news. Some nasty terrorist group has made some rather blood dripping threats. Apparently they hate the family of the Arabian drivers and want them erased from the face of the earth. There have been findings of Anthrax in some sugar cubes sent for the competitors. Lothar wasn’t exaggerating at all.”

Jason had to laugh. “I wonder if the ones who received those calls are able to differentiate between an Arabic accent and a German one?”

Isadora snickered. “Probably not. Lothar did really beat the big drum there”

Thor nodded and his eyes glittered. “Yes, but that is just good, nobody does question if the call was authentic or not.”

Jason relaxed against the back of the couch. “So, what are the plans?”

Thor took a deep breath. “I don’t think we can expect the visitor for the first two days. It takes time to get here and we already know that the culprit likes to be thorough. So we have time to prepare some surprises.”

Jason frowned. “I just worry about one thing”

Brent turned his head. “Yes?”

Jason sort of grunted. “Well, the culprit shot Anna, in cold blood. He doesn’t care about people at all, and I fear that he may not be alone”

Thor looked a bit surprised. “Based on what? He has been alone so far?”

Jason took a deep breath. “The crop duster. He must have rented that plane, and that tells me he has money. And a man with money can rent whatever he wants, including people with little to no scruples”

Brent looked a bit incredulous. “Rent somebody to help him kill some horses?”

Jason shook his head. “No, to create diversions.”

Isadora frowned. “That does imply that he knows he is expected doesn’t it?”

Jason shrugged. “Listen, I may be wrong but I am a cop, I am suspicious. That has saved my life so many times. I have an odd feeling here. This is a ranch after all, not some fancy racing stable. There are bound to be guns and even dogs here, and lots of toughened folks used to protecting themselves and their property. If I was that bastard I would take that into consideration"

Thor nodded and his expression became a thoughtful one. "I know, so I have made preparations, like I said. I have extra help coming inn tomorrow, at first light."

Jason looked a bit doubtful. "I hope it isn't the local redneck squad? Trigger happy gun-nuts is the last thing we need here"

Thor shook his head. "No, these are professionals. Just as professional as Lothar's men are. "

Isadora felt a bit curious, and shocked. "How come you know such men?"

Thor smiled. "Through dad, he fought in several wars, and got contacts. I have kept in touch with some of dad's old buddies and they in turn have contacts and…just wait and see!"

Isadora just shrugged. "Okay, but what are we to do today?"

Thor grinned with some pride. "I want to show you the place, and what we have done so far"

Jason looked eager but Brent made a sort of grimace, he looked almost apologetic. "Sorry, I think I want to stay here and be available for the groom, I am worried about Moon"

Thor nodded and smiled widely. "Of course, the living room has excellent reception and there is a good wi fi network here too. No password needed."

Brent grinned and looked relieved. "Great, I can make myself useful and go over those papers again"

Thor turned to Isadora. "I think you will like this place"

Jason tilted his head. “I hope your workers are ready to really get out there and protect the place?”

Thor nodded. “They are, most are armed and I have given them positions which they are to take when the time comes.”

He lead them out of the house through a backdoor and now they saw the stables behind the main house. They were rather large but not very high and the roofs were covered with turf. Thor smiled. “It is a good trick, keeps the warmth inn in winter and out during summer”

Jason stared at the roofs. “And they are not easy to light on fire”

Thor nodded. “That too, if my workers do remember to water the roofs every now and then that is”

The first stable was massive, but there weren’t that many horses inn there. Just about twenty and Thor smiled. “I keep most of my horses out on the pastures most of the time, it is way better for them and they have vast areas to run around in.”

Jason stared at the horses, he did look a bit nervous. “Are these sports horses?”

Thor grinned. “Most are gonna be used for sports but they are young and under training. There are only a few here which are finished with their training”

He walked over to a box where a rather lean looking horse stood chewing some hay lazily. “This is Coyote Jack, he is a very good cattle horse but he is on stable rest, injured his left hock some weeks ago”

The horse just continued to chew his hay and didn't even look at them. Isadora knew that a cattle horse had to be very level headed to be able to do its job. Thor presented them to several of the other animals there, all had a promising future as everything from jumpers to barrel racers. There were several breeds there, even a very stocky animal which had to be some sort of crossbreed. It was the chef's horse, used during the harvest season to carry sacks of nuts back to the farm. The chef was fond of using local ingredients and would create superb food from just simple things.

Thor stopped in front of a barn where they kept vehicles, he did start two ATV's and Jason was given one as he mounted the other, telling Isadora to get up behind him. they drove out onto a narrow gravel road and Thor told them about the ranch and its history as they passed by several pastures and holts of trees. Apparently Thor's grandfather had bought the area and his father had expanded it and now it was a very large property. But there was a fence around it and it was a bit odd. Isadora did see that there were gates here and there and those were very solid. In fact they looked as if they could hold out a tank. Thor nodded at her and Jason. "You are not being fooled by your eyes. The gates are extremely solid"

Jason wetted his lips. "Why?"

Thor made a nasty grimace and Isadora could sense that he tensed up quite a bit. "Poachers. We have had a huge problem with that. They do drive along the back roads and crash the gates. But we put an end to that"

Isadora frowned. “But the fences aren’t as solid as the gates? Won’t they just drive through the fence instead?”

Thor grinned and his eyes shone. “Well thought Isadora, we did have a few cases of that and one of my workers did come up with the solution”

He stopped the vehicle and walked over to one of the poles holding the thick wire. “See? This is wood but there is a steel pole inserted into it. And it has an L shape, with some of the bottom facing out from the pasture”

Jason looked as if he had seen the light. “Aha, so when the poachers try to drive through the fence the car pushes the pole over and the bottom rises and bang, no more engine?”

Thor snickered and it did sound ominous. “Exactly, the steel is special made, a tungsten alloy, and if they have enough speed it will go through the entire engine block. It was a heck of a job placing the poles here but they are solid, and we don’t need to repair the fence that often at all”

Isadora giggled. “I bet that is a bit of a disappointment”

Thor nodded and smiled at her. “Oh yes, some have tried to get into the area on foot, we cannot stop that but we have dogs and they are allowed to roam free and there are cameras everywhere, they are motion triggered so they record whenever they sense something passing by. “

Jason frowned. “And that means that you must have a surveillance room?”

Thor nodded. “Yes, even more advanced than those of many casinos. Not a bunny can hop out here without me being aware of it.”

They got back onto the ATV’s and drove off again, Isadora felt oddly at ease, the area was gorgeous and she felt that she would have loved to stay there, for a long time. They passed by a river with water so clear it was almost invisible and some ponds which were teeming with tiny fish. It was a paradise and Jason also looked enthralled by the sights. “Goddamn it, I thought I was happy working in the city but man, if you ever need an extra hand do call me. This is Eden!”

Thor just grinned widely. “The roads have pressure sensors, if somebody does drive they will register the weight of the vehicle and the speed. There are also some drones hidden here and there, remotely controlled of course. I think we have it all ready”

Jason nodded, his face revealed that he was impressed indeed. “Yeah, and with that many armed people here I don’t think anybody would manage to do much harm”

Isadora frowned. “But I worry about planes and helicopters, and your horses are outdoors aren’t they?”

Thor looked at her and his eyes were gentle. “You fear something like that massacre down south don’t you?”

She had to grin and he took her hand, it felt comforting. “Do not worry, the airport will warn us and the guards have night vision goggles. They will see it if somebody tries to fly inn, even with a helicopter. And I will hide every horse here.”

She tried to smile but the worry was still there. They were heading down into a shallow but wide valley now and there was a barn there, close to some huge fir trees. It looked very old but solid and they stopped in front of it. “This barn was used to store all sorts of things, I have removed the structures on the inside and turned it into a shelter for the horses”

The barn doors were removed, it was just a huge opening and the interior was dark. The barn had to be very well made for there couldn’t be any gaps between the logs. “My grandfather supposedly stored liquor here during the prohibition, I am not so sure that it was true but I know they stored molasses here. You can still smell it”

Isadora got off the vehicle and sniffed discretely, yes, it was most definitely the smell of molasses. She suddenly noticed movement within the darkness and squealed, whatever it was, it was massive and she feared it was a bear. Thor grinned and laughed and waved his hand while whistling. The ground started to shake slightly. “Petite, it is me, come boy”

Isadora gaped, what came into the light had to be the most massive horse she had ever seen, she hadn’t even believed that a horse could be that huge. It had to be at least half shire and the massive head with a pair of very gentle eyes hovered way above even Thor. Jason was having eyes like tea cups and he was blinking. “Ah…what the heck is that thing?”

Thor did walk over and petted the horse on the chest, the animal was pitch black except from a tiny blaze and it was rather long haired and didn't look very tame at all. But it obviously was. "This is Petite, or Pete as people here prefer to call him. Who knows who gave him that silly name but we have gotten used to using it"

Isadora frowned. "Is he yours?"

Thor shrugged. "Pete doesn't belong to anybody, he comes and goes as he likes. There are gates for the animals in places where you cannot drive a car. You can put a harness on him and he'll work hard but you cannot just place him in a stable. "

Jason was still blinking. "But he is…humongous"

Thor nodded. "Yeah, I did measure him once, and he should be in the Guinness record book as the tallest horse but I don't want to make him famous, he is an elderly chap and should enjoy his golden years in peace. He keeps the area safe and keeps an eye on the other horses so I am glad he is here. And to what he is, I think he is half Belgian draft and half Shire, I am not sure but it is believable. He just showed up fifteen years ago and has stayed since"

Isadora dared to walk closer and the massive animal lowered its head and sniffed her, she found that she liked this horse a lot. "Can he be ridden?"

Thor made a sort of scoff. "If you can keep your balance trying to sit on something that wide yes, he won't throw you but he isn't a comfortable ride by far. He does his job here and that is all I ask of him"

Jason came a little closer to. "He protects the area? How?"

Thor pointed at the massive front legs. “He does chase off anything dangerous, I have seen him kill both wolves and coyotes and one of my workers found a dead bear he swore Pete here had killed. He is a stallion so it is his instinct to protect the herds”

Isadora stared up at the huge head and she knew that some horses are like that, capable of killing to protect their mares and foals. She didn’t doubt that this giant was capable of kicking a bear to death.

Thor smiled and scratched the massive chest again, the horse was shaking with joy and Isadora saw that he really trusted the man. “He is the gentlest horse you can imagine, like a kitten with my workers. We have used him to babysit everything from orphan calves to puppies and he has even looked after the kids of some of the workers, and he does it with pride and dedication. He will protect anything small and defenceless. He has a heart the size of the ocean this one, but threaten his herd and you are in trouble.”

They did take off again and they were shown a lot of very gorgeous places, there were herds of horses almost everywhere there and Isadora saw that they were mixed to say the least. Some herds were warmbloods, probably very valuable show horses while other herds did consist of everything from ponies to old plough horses. Thor did obviously adopt everything he could get his hands on.

When they returned to the ranch they hadn’t seen more than a wee bit of it and Thor smiled widely. “I would love to take you north to see the area where we keep the cattle but it is a rather long trek and we would need to ride horses, not ATV's. The cattle doesn't like the sound of engines at all"

Isadora looked a bit disappointed. "Oh, I had hoped to go for a ride, this area is so gorgeous"

Thor hesitated for a second. Then he nodded and smiled. "Right, know what? I am just gonna check with the other guys here, then we can take a short trip?"

Jason scoffed. "Pardon me but you will never get me up on a horse, no way! I think I will stay here and try to get the latest news from my bosses"

Thor shrugged but looked eager. "That is alright. Isadora?"

She nodded. "I am inn, just get me a horse who isn't too flighty"

Thor was beaming, he did appear to really like the idea of going for a ride. "I will notify the stable right away. Go get dressed"

Isadora did return to her room and found that there was a pair of riding pants there and boots too. She felt more like herself when she emerged from the room, she was wearing her usual outfit now. Thor was already waiting for her, he was also wearing riding clothes and held two horses by the reins. It was a very tall roan gelding and an elegant mare which had to be a purebred Arabian. She was a bluish grey and absolutely lovely. Isadora did gasp with sheer admiration and Thor handed her the reins. "This is Cher Ami, she is a perfect lady if you go gentle on her"

Isadora had to grin, "And if I don't?"

Thor tilted his head. "She'll turn into dynamite, believe me"

He got in the saddle of the gelding and petted him on the neck, "Rocky here is a former steeplechaser, he did alright but was just too lazy so I bought him. A very steady horse, and not afraid of anything"

He turned the horse towards the gate. "Follow me, I have some interesting stuff to show you"

Isadora was thrilled to be back on a horse again, the mare was smaller than Adagio but she was indeed dynamite, she could feel all that penned up energy and knew that she had to be very careful. A horse like that was prone to just explode into action if you asked for it and she knew enough of horses to know that this mare would love to turn it into a race.

The trail they followed did lead into another valley, wide and fertile with lots of trees and a river and Isadora squinted, she could have sworn that she saw something metallic shining there? As they got closer she was sure, there had to be metal there but it was moving? She gasped as she saw that source of the strange reflections, it was horses. Horses which shone like metal, silver, gold, copper and brass. She turned to Thor. "Don't tell me you have Akhal-tekes?"

Thor grinned from one ear to the other. "Forty three of them actually. My dad bought ten good mares and two stallions from Turkmenistan thirty years ago and this is the result"

Isadora had seen a few of the rare breed before, they were superb sports horses but very head strong and they did look peculiar with long slender necks, heads held extremely high and a body which did resemble that of a greyhound. Thor did point at the stallion leading the herd. "I plan on using them for endurance riding, they beat even Arabians in that sport"

Isadora nodded. "Yeah, I bet!"

She was enthralled by the beauty of these animals and a yearling filly ran alongside them for a few hundred yards, it was as if those hooves didn't even touch the ground. Thor saw her facial expression and his smile was wide and loving. They rode on and she was entertained by tales from the everyday at the ranch, some stories were funny and others tragic and she felt completely at ease there. The day was coming to an end soon and they were turning back towards the ranch now, following another river back uphill. Cher Ami had been a very well behaved one until now but suddenly the mare started acting up, she was snorting and pawing the ground and Isadora shortened the reins, the mare grunted and bucked and Isadora lifted her head up and tried to calm her down but to no prevail. Rocky too started to act up and Thor looked tense all of a sudden. "Dismount, they have caught the scent of something"

Isadora was about to get off the mare when the animal just spun around and she was tossed out of balance and fell. Luckily the horse didn't step on her but she had to let go of the reins and the mare took off, running up the trail with impressive speed. Thor swore and let go of Rocky, the gelding followed the mare and he ran over to Isadora. "Are you alright?"

She felt like laughing, she hadn't fallen like that since she was a young girl and she accepted Thor's outreached hand. He pulled and she let out a yelp, something stung her and she turned around, trying to see what it was. Thor grasped her and lifted her back onto her feet, very gently and he made a grimace. "Ah Isadora, you landed on a small cactus"

She had to laugh, it was comical "A cactus?"

He nodded and looked concerned. "The nasty type, the spines have gone through your pants"

She tried to walk but darn, it did sting, badly. "Is it dangerous? I mean, it could be bears here?"

Thor shook his head. "Nope, I bet they caught the scent of old Willy, the horses hate that scent"

Isadora had to frown again. "Old Willy?"

Thor looked a bit aspirated. "Yeah, an old boar, massive beast. He does some damage here but we haven't managed to get a shot at him, he is too old and too tough so I bet he wouldn't be useable for anything except soup"

Isadora scoffed, she knew that horses hate the smell of pigs. Thor sighed. "The horses will return to the stable and they will send someone for us. It is embarrassing though, I haven't just lost my horse like that since I was a kid"

Isadora grinned and tilted her head. "It is very hard to imagine you as a kid"

Thor laughed out loud. “But I was, believe me. My mom’s greatest worry, just legs and arms and little to no brains and later on pimples and bad smells and a nasty temper”

She had to giggle. “I see, I was a bit of a Tomboy, hated dolls and such things. I only wanted to ride ponies and pretend to be some fantasy heroine”

Thor cocked his head. “I can see that. But back to serious business, we need to get those spikes out, they can cause infections”

Isadora swallowed. “Ah, you cannot just pull them out?”

He sighed. “I can try, I have a Leatherman here, one second”

There was a pair of pliers within the multi tool he retrieved from his pockets and he took a deep breath. “Right, turn around and bend over”

Isadora had to giggle, a bit nervously. “That would have sounded absolutely kinky was the setting different”

Thor blushed a bit, but he did kneel and got the tool ready. Isadora felt like an idiot, landing on a cactus, it was truly really embarrassing. He grasped onto the first spine and pulled and Isadora squeaed, it hurt like hell and it felt as if the cactus spine was stuck. “Ow, no, it doesn’t work”

Thor looked apologetic. “Hmm, ah, sorry, but …you need to try to pull your pants down”

She sent him a glare. “What?”

He looked down. "The fabric, it is too dense. The spines are caught in it. If you pull the pants off you may be able to pull the spines from your skin, all in one go"

Isadora swallowed hard. Bearing her butt to someone wasn't something she had done in a very long time. "I see…well"

She took a deep breath, right, so the most gorgeous man in the history of mankind was about to take a good peek at her arse. No big deal right? No pressure? She hadn't shaved her legs for what had to be a small lifetime and her bikini line? Oh it was a disaster. It was enough to make her blush like a field of beets. She took a deep breath, at least her underpants would stay on, hopefully…

She grasped the lining of the riding pants and pushed them down but had to stop, it simply hurt too much. "Ow, ow, oh shit. I cannot do it"

Thor had a very odd expression within his eyes, part amusement and part compassion. "They have to come out, there could be an hour or two before we are picked up"

He got up and then he suddenly kissed her on her brow, she was stunned by the sudden action and then he bent down very fast and pulled her pants down, all the way. Isadora yelled and felt tears filling her eyes but the pants were out of the way and he turned her around and took a look at her butt. "There are just a few spines left, brilliant"

She panted, she was completely bare and it hurt and she felt so horribly exposed. He look edup at her. "I am so very sorry Isa, but for each minute those spines are inn there the chance of infection does increase. I have seen it before, and believe me, the boils are nasty"

She swallowed. "Right, get the rest out"

He just nodded and started pulling. It was easier now and he was done in just a couple of minutes. There was some blood on her skin and he pulled her underwear back on but the pants were still filled with nasty spines. "You will have to get rid of those"

She didn't know if she was to cry or laugh. "So I am to return to the ranch without my pants? Now that isn't going to get rumours started..,"

Thor got back up and his eyes were very sincere. "Nobody will speak an ill word of you Isadora, I…"

He looked down and there was a sort of conflict visible within his eyes. "I have something to confess to you…"

He looked up again. "But I don't know if I dare to…"

Isadora blushed, she had seen the signs and she hadn't dared to believe them. "I think I already know"

He took a deep breath. "You do? What…what do you think of it.."

She leaned forth and then she kissed him, gently but with some pressure and he moaned and suddenly she was held rather firmly and she was being kissed in a manner she hadn't even dared to imagine in her wildest dreams. It made her toes curl up and it felt just perfect, just right. She grasped onto him and answered the kiss and he moaned and pulled her even closer and she had to moan too, her body suddenly felt as if it was on fire. She had never experienced desire like this before and right now she didn't care if they ended up in the bushes, she wanted him, more than she wanted air.

He was lifting her shirt and started kissing her breasts through the bra and she started working on his belt. It was stuck, the buckle a rather intricate one and she groaned with frustration and felt him shiver. "Oh Isa, I have wanted this for so long, you are perfect, so lovely"

He kissed her neck and shoulder and Isadora gasped and cursed her sore butt, if they were to do it now they would have to do it standing up, or with her on top. Thor was panting and his eyes were so very dark, it was the most interesting sight she had seen for a long time. Her last relationship had been more than ten years ago and it had been a short one, she had realized that Benjamin had been dating her just to use her as a springboard for his own career. And so she had dumped him rather crassly. But this…she palmed him through his pants and felt that he indeed was very interested and also quite well endowed. He gasped and closed his eyes and he was panting. "Isa, if you do that again…"

He grasped her hand and kissed it. "These pants will need to be washed"

She giggled and licked her lips. "Then get rid of them"

He kissed her again, almost desperately. "Yes, oh Isa"

She knew she was ready for just about anything now and she did want this, more than anything. She had skin hunger for sure, and she had simply ignored her own needs for years now. That was not very wise, her feelings were spiralling out of control, with racer speed. He started opening his belt, then he suddenly took a deep breath and grasped her chin, kissed her again. “Isa, ah…are you on something?”

She frowned. “What? On something?”

He nodded, eyes black and breath heavy. “Birth control, anything? “

She let out a curse. “No, I…oh damnation, I want you Thor, so very badly”

He leaned his forehead against hers. She felt him tremble. “Likewise, I won’t be able to stop if we go any further now, and…I don’t want to cause you trouble”

She sighed. “I know, you are too honourable aren’t you? Oh crap, we’ll have to wait”

He tried to smile. “I have condoms somewhere in my flat. But they may be old”

Isadora felt embarrassed but she felt something else too. Respect. Not all men would have thought about that, most would have given absolutely zero fucks about it and gone ahead. He was truly well raised. “I tried the pill for a while but my body responded badly”

He took a deep breath. “Right, we have to…”

He closed his eyes. “We have to start walking, if we stay here I am sure we will be too sorely tempted”

She giggled. “So your condoms are old? Does that mean that the most sought after bachelor of the equine society is celibate?”

He nodded, still trembling. “My dad raised me very well, I do not run around screwing everything I see. I know that my looks and wealth can attract the wrong type of women”

She pulled the ruined pants off and he gallantly offered her his shirt, to tie around her waist like a sort of skirt. “Have you any experience with that?”

He nodded and made a grimace. “Yes, I met a girl just a year after my father died, I was in grief and very insecure and well, she knew how to play the game and play it well too. But mom saw through her, and exposed her for the gold digger she was.”

Isadora frowned. “Is your mother alive still?”

Thor shook his head, there was sorrow in his eyes. “No, she died two years ago, a rare form of cancer. “

Isadora sighed. “Too bad, she sounds like a smart woman”

He smiled widely. “She was, very smart and very wise. And a real she wolf when it came to protecting me”

Isadora started to walk, it felt odd for her butt was sore and she had that heavy feeling within her body still, she was still aroused and it was uncomfortable now that she knew that she wouldn’t be offered any release yet.

They walked slowly up the path, Isadora felt her cheeks burn, he was so devastatingly handsome and now she knew that he felt the same way as she did, it made it hard to resist. She was glad he had managed to stop though, she did fear that an unwanted surprise would have been quite possible. She knew her cycle and she couldn't be that far away from ovulation. She wanted kids but not yet, and not before she knew she was in a stable relationship.

Thor took her hand. "I hope they come to pick us up soon, I have a hard time walking"

Isadora had to laugh. "I can see that, you are wobbling"

He grinned and embraced her. "I love you, it is odd but I think I have for years, since I saw you for the first time, riding that huge gelding of yours down that embankment at the Crochton track, like you had a special deal made with gravity, absolutely fearless!"

She giggled and leaned her head against his shoulder. "Likewise, you were like Bellerophon, riding the Pegasus"

He laughed, a warm laugher. "Do not compare me with the gods Isa, that is never wise"

She just held onto the firm arm and hoped that they wouldn't have to walk that far until they were picked up.

They had made it back to the plain when they saw that somebody came driving towards them with a pick up. It was the ragged man who was named Joe and he didn't even raise an eyebrow at Isadora's odd clothing. She carried the pants over her shoulder, with cactus spines sticking out of it still and she had to kneel down on the seat instead of sitting on it. Her butt was really sore now. It was dark when they arrived and Thor carried her inside, nobody was there and he took her straight to his private rooms. They were grand, but also very personal and nice and she was placed on a bed. "Stay here, I will go get Adriene, she can fix those sores."

Isa was disappointed, she had wanted him to take care of it but no such luck. He left and she laid there on her belly, feeling odd. Thor returned with the elderly woman and she carried a box with some sorts of ointment in it and some bandages. She clicked her tongue and sat down next to Isadora. "Bad luck ha? I know those spines, nasty nasty things"

She took some ointment onto a piece of bandage and wiped Isadora's rear with it, very gently. It stung but Isadora felt that it was perhaps the best thing, for it would clean the wounds and prevent scars. Thor had been in Isadora's room and got her some new underwear and Adriene grinned and snickered, she was obviously aware of what was going on. "Now you two young things, the lady does need to rest for a couple of days so no fun until then"

Isadora had to grin. "Right, not what I wanted to hear but alright"

Thor gave her a hug. "But you will stay here with me still? I want to spoil you"

She nodded. "The horses were alright when they arrived?"

He smiled and rubbed her shoulders. "Yes, both were fine. And Jason and Brent has worked rather well too, they made a lot of calls and it is confirmed now, the culprit did indeed disguise himself as a farrier."

Isadora swallowed, back to the stark reality again. "Okay, so, what now?"

Thor did shrug. "We wait, simple as that. My workers have warned every ranch in the area and the village to the south of here too. If some stranger do show up we'll be alerted."

She sighed. "Right, the waiting game. It is the most boring and nerve wreaking game ever invented. "

He laid down next to her on the bed. "Yes, but I know how to spend the time well. I have ordered some food and wine and then you are gonna get a good bath before bedtime"

She had to giggle. "I cannot wait"

The chef had to be convinced that they were about to die from hunger for the meal was enough to feed four adult men, and the wine was just the right temperature and Isadora knew she couldn't drink more than one glass before she got tipsy. Jason and Brent were invited to join them and Isadora sat on a soft pillow and had to tell them how she managed to land on a cactus several times. Brent was laughing and Jason cringed each time she mentioned it. They spent some time playing poker and Brent cheated with bravado. They did in fact have a good time, the ointment had taken away some of the pain and she felt way better now that she was dressed again. Brent wouldn't have cared if she sat there in her nickers but Jason would probably have developed some problems.

Thor helped her take a warm bath and then he helped her to bed, regretting that he couldn't join her in bed for if he did he wouldn't be able to keep his hands to himself.

Isadora felt a bit flattered by his words and they kissed before he left to his own bedroom. He did confess that he probably wouldn't be sleeping at all, at least not to begin with.

Isadora was tired and she fell asleep fast and she didn't dream at all. She was awakened by Thor, he was kissing her brow and held a cup of hot coffee. "Wake up, I have breakfast ready and my reinforcements are coming soon"

She got up and got dressed, her hair was a tangled mess and Thor brushed it and braided it for her. It was very obvious that he was very fond of spoiling his loved ones. After breakfast they left the building and Isadora was still very sore, her butt ached and it was a bit swollen too. Thor had checked and there wasn't any signs of infection, it was just that the tissue had become irritated.

They were chatting away as they waited, the sun was rising and it was such a very lovely sight and Isadora had fallen in love with the ranch by now, it was such a wonderful place. They were contemplating going back inside when a huge truck pulled into the yard. It was carrying the mark of a feed brand and some huge corn cobs and straws of wheat were drawn onto the sides of it. Thor smiled at the confused faces. "If the culprit is already here somewhere a feed truck won't seem suspicious at all"

The driver backed up towards one of the stables where it was rather dark still and opened the back door. Several men exited, all carrying equipment and they did all seem as if they were ready to fight a world war. The leader was a man who did look a bit like Thor, he was very tall and elegant and had long blonde hair but his eyes were grey and he had a harsh face with some scars which had to have come from burns. He did bow his head. “Thor, I brought my best men”

Thor shook his hand. “Wonderful, I am afraid we’ll need them”

The man stared at the others there. “Are they prepared?”

Thor nodded. “Yes, do not worry.”

Jason cocked his head. “I am sure I have seen you before Sir?”

The man nodded. “I was the leader of a rather high profile case some years ago yes, a kidnapping”

Jason blinked. “The Bloomberg/Atchkins case? That was a mess”

The blonde smiled, a very narrow smile. “Yes, but we got the victim out without her getting injured. The kidnapper on the other hand…”

Jason just nodded slowly, there was respect in his eyes and Isadora realized that he knew more about this man than they did, except Thor of course. The men walked into the stable and the truck left, Isadora saw that they carried many boxes of equipment and they used an empty box as a command centre. The blond didn’t give any orders, it was very clear that everybody knew what to do and when.

Jason was checking his gun, he still carried the Beretta he had gotten from Lothar and he had a grim expression on his face. “I spoke with my boss some hours ago, they have done a total count at those racing stables. Thirty people are dead, ten more injured."

Isadora knew why so few were injured compared with the ones who had died, the fire had been too fast and too hot for anybody to survive, the ones who were injured were the ones caught at the outskirts of the blaze, they had tried to run away. Jason put the gun back in its holster. "The number of dead horses is also staggering. The bastard must feel so proud of himself"

The blond soldier smiled, it wasn't a nice smile. "Right, we are dealing with a very dangerous individual. I would recommend that you all stay close to the buildings from now on and don't go out there alone. The worst thing which can happen is for one to be taken as a hostage"

Jason shrugged. "He haven't bothered with that before?"

The blond nodded sternly and the eyes were flint hard. "No, but that can change. Never take anything for granted when it comes to such people. They are like rabid animals. "

Thor grimaced and Brent looked rather nervous. "But we will be safe in here right?"

The soldier nodded. "I cannot see why not, if that monster is after the horses first and foremost he will try to attack the stables, or the herds"

Thor nodded. "I have men all over the place, hidden. They are ready to roll"

The soldier smiled that nasty smile. “Good, and tell them to shoot first and ask questions later, you cannot risk any mistakes now”

Thor sighed. “I know, we will be alert”

Isadora took a peek at the buildings, all were made from wood and she cringed. “What if he try to use that same trick again?”

The soldier bowed his head. “We have drones in the air, he will have to use a helicopter or a propeller plane, a jet is too fast. And no plane can fly without its propeller”

Isadora felt a bit faint. “You will crash a drone into the propeller?”

The soldier nodded sternly. “Won’t be the first time. Also, helicopters do not fly well with their rotor blades sheared off”

She took a deep breath “Well Mr, I am sure that you are well prepared”

The soldier grinned, a more gentle grin this time. “It is Ty Ma’am, Ty Nolan, and yes, we are experts, we are always prepared”

Thor patted her on her back. “Listen and relax dear, I trust my coworkers, and I trust these guys”

Brent did look nervous still. “I would evacuate the horses, just to be on the safe side”

Thor smiled at him. “That is being arranged, they are to be moved today. I have a hidden stable down the valley”

Brent frowned. “A hidden stable?”

Thor nodded. “It was my grandfather’s idea you see, it wasn’t built as a stable but as a shelter, in case of a nuclear war.”

Isadora had to stare at him. “Seriously?”

Thor nodded. “The old fart was paranoid and extremely loud when it came to politics, he made many enemies and I think he did build the place more due to the neighbours than a real threat from the soviets. But it is there, and rather nice too”

Brent still looked a bit confused. “How do you hide a stable?”

Thor grinned. “It was a cave, in the cliff side. It is very well hidden, the entrance cannot be found unless you are aware of it and the old man expanded it a lot. It can house a town now, for months”

Brent grunted. “That is great, but do it before sunset, nobody should see that you evacuate the horses”

Thor just grinned and Isadora had an odd feeling at the bottom of her chest, as if she was short of breath. She was genuinely frightened, not just for the horses but for the safety of Thor and herself too. It would be too bad if they were to lose each other now, when they just had discovered the feelings they were sharing.

The day was spent watching how the workers did bring the horses from the stables down into the valley, Isadora and Brent helped out and she did discover that Brent had a wicked sense of humour and that he was also capable of organizing things very fast. She learned that he had met his partner in an art gallery of all things and that Joel was an artist working with glass and metal. He was rather famous and created some rather incredible sculptures. Thor was placing people around the fence and within the ranch too and it was obvious that many locals too had shown up, eager to show their support and help out.

The dinner that day was eaten in groups and everybody was busy. The chef was making baskets for the workers to bring with them and Thor hoped that this would be over soon, it did interfere with the normal daily routine. The people taking care of the pigs hardly had time to feed them and the ones guarding the cattle had to reduce their numbers from five to two.

Isadora realized that Thor had a very large wine cellar, and it was filled with very expensive wines from all over the world. He even had some types of liquor which was hard to come by. She got curious about a rather large red bottle and he let her pick it off the shelf. It was liquor made from arctic crow berries and was named Frost and he had gotten it from a friend who visited Norway. She had a taste and it was good but very sweet and Thor reveal ed that he used to mix it with Schweppes lemon, that made it perfect. Brent was in awe of the wine cellar, he was a connoisseur and the two men sat there discussing wine until it got rather late. By then Isadora was tipsy and she felt as if she was floating. Her butt hurt still and that was a darn pity for Thor was absolutely toothsome in those tight jeans and a dark t shirt. She cursed that goddamn cactus yet again.

They went to bed and the house went quiet, the guards were out there and the soldiers kept an eye on their equipment. The workers were ready too and Thor had his phone next to his bed, just in case the airport should call. The night went by in silence and when the sun did rise again nothing had happened. The only thing which had transpired was that one of the volunteers had tripped and twisted his ankle. The hidden stable was so large the workers could allow the horses to move around a bit and they were exercised during the day. Isadora and Brent and Jason was treated to a round trip of the entire ranch, from outside the fences and they drove a rather large jeep which had what could only be described as pre historic springs. Isadora had a feeling that her arse had been through a grinder, it hurt and felt sore and she wished that she could have grasped that cactus and turned it into something useful, like a shot of tequila.

But the trip took much of the day and Isadora was a bit annoyed that she and Thor didn't manage to get any time on their own, she longed to be alone with him but at the same time, she did enjoy the company of Brent and Jason. Brent was very worried now, he hadn't heard anything yet regarding Mr Berner and his plans for Crested Moon and Isadora was well aware of the possibility of his heir letting her daughter have the mare. Some people are stupid enough to believe that a top trained horse can bring their kids victories even if said kid is about as talented as a bag of wool. Thor tried to calm Brent down but he was constantly nervous and fidgety and even calls from Joel didn't calm him down. Isadora knew why, he was afraid that the girl would ruin Moon, and more so, that the kid would get hurt and that the mother would take it out on the horse.

Isadora and Thor promised him that if the woman refused to allow him to use the mare they would try to back him up, whatever way they could. Brent was very grateful. The day went by and the next night was also very quiet, the soldiers were alert all the time, they slept in turns and were ready for anything at all times. Jason acted as if he was some kid meeting his great idol each time he was around Ty and Isadora realized that the large man was somewhat famous for some reason. She felt tempted to google the name but she had a feeling that a search would come up empty. Such professionals do not allow themselves to become too well known. Thor just said that they had to be patient and Isadora tried to listen to him. they watched movies and reruns of the competitions they had competed inn and Isadora did speak to her uncle a few times. The body of Adagio had been buried by now and she was in a way glad she hadn't seen him after the fire. Thor was right, she remembered him as he had been that evening, relaxed and happy.

It was three days before anything happened and it was in the late evening. The sun was setting and the small group was sitting on the patio outside of the main building when a car appeared along the road leading to the ranch. It was an old car, a typical farm vehicle built to haul everything from fencing wire to live cattle and hay bales and it was so worn and old it did resemble a rust bucket more than a car. It was a bit of a miracle it could move. The engine sputtered and coughed and the transmission sounded like some poor sinners soul being tormented in purgatory. It made Isadora want to cover her ears. An elderly man more or less fell out of the car, he was wearing tattered and dirty clothes and his hair and moustache was greasy and stiff. Thor however smiled towards the man who had a severe limp, he had a sort of dignity which made him look like a person you ought to listen to, even if he did look like a bum. “A good evening to you Hemie, what brings you to my not so humble abode?”

The old man snickered and Isadora realized that it was an old joke between Thor and this man. Hemie shrugged. “I just came to tell you that I have some disturbing news, certain individuals have disappeared from the town”

Thor frowned and gestured for Hemie to sit down, the old man got a can of beer and looked like a very happy camper there and then. “Who?”

Hemie emptied the can with a speed that was nothing short of impressive. “Jake, and the Jonesby brothers, they disappeared yesterday according to Jonesy at the bar”

Thor had a very dark expression within his eyes. “That is not very good. That is not good at all.”

Jason had a bewildered expression upon his face. “What? What is going on?”

Thor sighed and leaned back into his chair. “Those men are the outcasts of this society, scumbags, drunks and addicts. They will do anything for a hit, and stop at nothing. If the bastard has managed to contact them they will be more than willing to do some dirty work for him”

Jason swallowed. “Do they know this place?”

Thor sighed and his face was ice cold. “Yes, they all have worked here, the only good thing about them is that they are dumber than a block of ice, Jake is the worst of them, he is sly and vicious”

Isadora shuddered and pulled her blanket tighter around her shoulders. “So, what can they do?”

Hemie grunted. “They can create a heck of a lot of problems, neither are good shots, and they are in terrible shape but I wouldn’t say that they won’t try to shoot somebody if they are given the chance to do it and get away with it. They hate everybody who has success, even the slightest hint of it. “

Thor nodded solemnly. “Jake was employed by my dad for a while, to work with the cattle but he did abuse the horses and was drunk most of the time. Dad kicked him out of here and he has hated this place ever since. He is a nasty piece of shit and spends most of his days in the town jail but he haven’t done anything so severe the sheriff can throw away the key, yet”

Jason frowned and picked up his phone. “Let me see if he does have a record outside of this county, what is his full name?”

Thor gave it and Jason went to work. Hemie looked at Isadora. “Your girlfriend Thor? Keep a very good eye on her, that son of a bitch will target her if he thinks she is yours”

Thor looked nervous, and he grasped Isadora’s hand. “I won’t let that happen”

Isadora swallowed and felt cold to the core, so one madman wasn't enough, now they were bound to have to cope with three more.

Jason turned back to them and shut off his phone. "Guys, that guy has a wrap sheet as long as a roll of toilet paper. He is no good at all"

Thor sort of grunted and made a grimace, the blue eyes were rather sharp. "No surprise there really. Jake is the kind of man who would sell off his own mother for a cag of booze."

Brent took a deep breath. "So, the culprit could possibly have hired these three? Then he must have been here for a few days, or at least heard about the town. But we haven't heard from the airport?"

Thor just nodded. "He must have driven inn after all, and driven fast too."

Hemie shrugged, he smelled of leather and horse dung and there were horse hairs on his jeans, he probably worked with animals. "The good people would have noticed if some stranger just showed up. Me thinks that he have called them"

Jason was suddenly a bit pale, his eyes got huge. "But how did he find their phone numbers? You don't get registered in the phone book as "Mr this or that, criminal" I know only one place where you can get that sorts of information about a person"

Thor snapped his fingers. "The police records?

Jason nodded and he opened his phone again, he looked as if he was in a fit of panic. "Right, the bastard has somehow gotten access to the criminal records of these individuals, and their contact information. He has to have either hacked the police or he has somebody working for him"

Isadora swallowed. "I think he has paid somebody, I mean, there are police officers who are willing to ignore the rules right? If the price is right?"

Brent pointed a finger at her. "There you have it, he must have managed to buy off somebody who knew the local population, and what they have been up to. Somebody within the police department"

Jason looked confused but Hemie tilted his head. "The junior depute, Josh Sinclair, he is really too stupid to be allowed to walk without the help of a walker. I tell ya, that man cannot chew bubblegum and walk at the same time, it makes his brain short out. But he works at the sheriff's office, and the sheriff does manage to keep his cools when the bastard fucks things up, he is the sheriff's wife's sister's son you see"

Thor turned to Jason. "Listen, call the Sheriff's office, see if you can reach the sheriff himself and tell them of our suspicions. If this Sinclair dude has been selling info he ought to be flogged and rolled in tar and feather"

Hemie grinned from one ear to the other. "Oh my, sheriff Baker will love this, a good excuse to finally get rid of that moron"

Jason grasped the phone and walked off. Isadora stared at Thor. "What are we to do? Can those three really pose a threat?"

Thor hesitated and his face was a bit distant. "Yes, I am sorry dear but they know the ranch and they know the terrain. And they have probably listened to the people here and know that we have guards out there, and surveillance. "

Brent bit his lower lip. "Listen, I know you won't like this Isadora but this evening? I suggest that she spends the night within that hidden stable. Do they know about it?"

Thor looked a bit worried. "Maybe? I don't know for sure but if they do it won't do them any good. The doors are extremely solid and can withstand a huge bomb. And there is no other way inn"

Isadora blinked and felt a bit conflicted. One part of her wanted to stay with Thor and Brent and the other part wanted to be safe, to hide from this danger. Thor smiled. "You are to stay in the stable tonight. If they left yesterday they could be anywhere by now, it is likely it will go down tonight"

Isadora let her breath out in a huge sigh. "Right, fine. I will stay there. But I do think I have an idea"

Brent smiled at her and his smile was a bit more relaxed now that she had agreed. "Alright, what sort of an idea?"

She pulled at her long mahogany hair. "If the bastard knows about me, and he may, he will anticipate a woman here. But he could suspect foul play if there isn't one. One of the men who followed Ty was very slender and about my height. A long wig on that one?"

Thor had to laugh. "Oh my…Yes, that is perfect. A good idea. I will speak to Ty right away."

He got up and disappeared and Hemie winked at her. “He is completely taken by you miss, and that is a good thing. He needs somebody in his life”

Isadora felt herself blushing. “Yeah, I guess. Pardon me asking but what do you work with?”

Hemie grinned widely. “I work for a neighbour, keeping an eye on his horses. I used to be a rodeo rider ya see. Old Olof could see I had talent and made it so I could compete. But I had an ugly fall some years ago and my knee never healed. Cannot ride anymore, but I can still drive a car and make myself useful”

Isadora understood and they sat there discussing horses when Thor returned with Ty and the man Isadora had mentioned. He did really look a bit like her from afar, as if he was her brother or something and he was grinning. The guy did look like an ordinary fellow but if he worked with Ty he was probably lethal and very well trained. He did scratch his head. “So, you want me to pose as Mr Oswold’s girlfriend? Shouldn’t be too hard really”

Thor had a wry expression on his face. “If the culprit did contact the three before people around here became aware of the danger he haven’t been told that we are expecting him. He will probably go for the weakest link in the chain and that would be Isadora”

Isadora scoffed. “I am not weak!”

Thor smiled at her. “Absolutely not dear, but others may think so.”

Jason came sprinting back inside of the patio, he was waving his phone. “I got in touch with the sheriff. The idiot received a phone call the very day after we arrived here, when the driving competition got cancelled. It was somebody claiming to be a reporter, making a case about the crime rates of rural areas and the jerk had a very loose tongue and told everything about the criminals of this parish. He is not working for the sheriff anymore, that is for darn certain. If he manages to get a job scrubbing plates at the local fast food restaurant that would be a miracle.”

Hemie snickered and his eyes got narrow. “Sheriff Baker told him a few truths?”

Jason was laughing. “Ah, I would say that the guy got the verbal beating of this century. He broke all the rules in one go. But now we know how the culprit got the names, he wants to create a diversion for sure”

Thor nodded. “I will warn everybody, tell them to change their positions. But they have to be discrete about it. “

He kissed Isadora on her brow. “And you are to be safe within the stable, that makes me way more at ease”

Hemie got up. “I better get going, I am needed back home but good luck to ya. I fear that the bastards will strike today”

The soldier was standing there next to Ty and the two were discussing something very quietly. Ty turned to Thor “Here is what we’ll do. The culprit will most certainly go for the horses first and foremost, when he finds no horses here he will become confused, then he will become angry. He will be off balance, unable to think.

From what I have seen this person needs to be in control, to plan ahead. He is a perfectionist but driven by his hatred, yet he wants his vengeance to be perfect."

Thor nodded slowly and crossed his arms over his chest. "So, what are we to do then?"

Ty turned to the younger man. "Frank here will don some lady's clothing, and a wig and some make up. A little stuffing in front and nobody will see that he isn't a woman, at least not from afar. But he will be armed, and so will you Thor. You will all be wearing protection"

He opened a bag he had carried with him and pulled out some bullet proof vests. "You will wait until we have contact confirmed, then you will leave the ranch, with "miss" here. And if I am not completely mistaken the culprit will follow, simply to get even"

Thor snickered. "The disappointment will make him snap?"

Ty nodded solemnly. "Yes, I know how such depraved people think, I have come across them oh so many times. Some turn to religion and becomes the kind of hypocrite who loves to tell others how terrible they are and others again become obsessed with some obscure and radical line of ideas and becomes terrorist. And in common is that they are completely convinced that they are in the right and everybody else is wrong and out to get them"

Brent looked as if he was tasting something horrible. "So what are we others doing?"

Ty made a small grimace. “You are to escort Miss Singer to the stable and stay there with her, I recon that you have more people in there Thor?”

Thor nodded. “At least ten workers yes”

Ty smiled. “Good. Now, Jason, you are a good shot?”

Jason shrugged. “Good or good, I am not so sure, I am decent?”

Ty tilted his head and those grey eyes were like flint again. “Doesn’t matter much, you are to become a distraction of needed. To give cover.”

He took out a map and laid it on the table. “Here, the old barn north of here, you and Frank will head that way, slowly. The culprit will follow, and Jason and I will take cover here”

He pointed at an outcrop not far from the barn. “It gives me the perfect position”

Thor swallowed. “Do you want to kill him?!”

Ty shook his head .”No, I can if I have to but I do have something special in store”

Brent got curious. “What?”

Ty just grinned and the grin was one which would make everybody’s bones feel cold. “Non lethal weapons are the rage these days, I have the very best. He won’t die, but he sure as hell will wish he did”

Thor checked his watch. “Right, it is already getting late. Brent, Isadora. You go get whatever you need for the night, I will send one of the workers with you. “

Frank did grin. “I will go and get ready too, I love such missions”

Ty threw the guy a kiss and he did toss his head back in a coquettish manner with a pout. It was obvious that these men knew each other very well and could joke and have fun even when things were grave.

Isadora and Brent hurried to find clothes and other things they needed and when they returned one of the ranch workers stood there with a small car normally used to transport injured calves. It did stink of manure but if somebody were watching it wouldn’t look out of place at all. Brent and Isadora managed to squeeze themselves into the back and the driver grinned. “Hold on, the road is a bit bumpy. I will drive slowly but some of the pot holes are bad”

Isadora saw that Frank too had returned.

Now he wore a flimsy summer dress and a jacket and he had a long wig which did resemble Isadora’s hair at least to some degree. He couldn’t be mistaken as a woman from close distance but in the dark it was very possible to think he was Isadora. Ty was gone and so was Jason, they were going to their positions and Isadora felt her heart racing as they drove off. She was very nervous on behalf of Thor, she just hoped that the tall blonde wouldn’t be harmed in any way.

The stable was indeed very well hidden, the doors camouflaged and whence they were closed you couldn’t even see that they were there. The worker found a panel and pushed some buttons and a small door slid open, wide enough for a person to pass through but not more than that. He smiled at them. “Good luck, you are safe here”

Isadora took a deep breath. There was a long corridor leading into the mountain side before they reached the stable and Brent grunted and looked uncomfortable. “This is like Cheyenne mountain, I hate being in caves”

Isadora had to laugh at his miserable expression. “I am sure that it is perfectly safe”

The giant room they entered was divided into several departments and in some there were boxes with horses and others were open corrals with horses running free. Isadora saw that Thor had brought all the herds into this place, even some mustangs which were held in corrals with very tall fences. The ground was covered with a mixture of sand and sawdust and everything was clean and in order. Some workers were busy taking care of the animals and Brent saw that there were rooms ready for the workers there too. He and Isadora was shown to one each by a very friendly young woman who confessed that she had been working on this ranch for five years and that it had been awesome.

Isadora did walk over to where the akhal-teke’s were kept, the strange horses were fascinating and the stable worker responsible for them did greet her and smiled. “You like them?”

Isadora did nod and Brent was also very fascinated. “These are excellent for all sorts of sports yes?”

The worker nodded. “They are brave, and their endurance is extreme”

Isadora stared at the metallic coats and sighed in admiration, a horse like that would turn heads, just the same way a Lamborghini did. The worker did wink. “You are an eventer aren’t you?”

Isadora swallowed hard. “Ah, yes, I…I lost my horse in that fire. I need a horse who can both jump and do dressage, it isn’t easy to find”

The worker looked very smug. “Oh but I think we may have what you need then, in fact I think he may be perfect”

She turned around. “Follow me”

Brent looked very curious too and followed the two, they entered an area of boxes which were extra solid, this was where the stallions were kept and Isadora was starting to wonder what this stable worker was up to. They stopped in front of a box and the man tilted his head and made a theatrical gesture “Let me present to you; Starfall”

Isadora could only gape. The horse in that box wasn’t like anything she had ever seen before, he was huge and elegant and the muscles in the arched neck and mighty hind quarters were like a coil of snakes under the thin hide. But the odd thing was the colour, he was black, and at the same time he was metallic golden. The colours shimmered and changed as the animal moved and Brent was gaping. “That is bloody impossible?!”

The worker was laughing. “No it isn’t, the boss has been breeding those Akhal teke’s for years and he has tried to mix the breed with others and sometimes you do strike gold. This one is most certainly gold, or rather platinum, or titanium. Precious for short"

Isadora was still gaping, the animal was exquisite, perfection. But he was very tall and she could see an almost eerie intelligence within the deep dark eyes. The worker smiled. "He can outrun almost anything, and fears nothing. This is one of the best horses we have ever bred"

Isadora blinked and swallowed. "What breeds is he?"

The worker shrugged. "Ah, I have no idea? The boss keeps his secrets but we know that the dam is a pure akhal teke, the sire on the other hand is anybody's guess. "

Brent was almost drooling. "He is magnificent. Why haven't Thor used him in competitions?"

The worker smiled again. "I think he was planning on starting this one when Silver Ghost got too old. Starfall is only eight, he is trained but not very experienced yet"

He was way more powerful looking than an akhal-teke, that was for sure. The elegant lines were there but they were more curved, it was like comparing a greyhound with an timber wolf. Isadora suddenly felt an odd feeling of something akin to hunger, to ride a horse like that…

Brent saw her expression and snickered. "Easy there girl, that horse looks as if he is a true handful"

She sighed. "I know, and I bet Thor will want to use him now that Silver Ghost is gone"

Brent rolled his eyes. “And the rest of us will be left in the dust, nobody will stand a chance against that beast”

The worker interrupted them. “There will be a meal served soon, and we will turn the lights down a bit to let the horses have some time to sleep.”

Isadora nodded. “I don’t think I will be able to sleep tonight”

Brent shook his head. “Me neither, I am glad I was sent here. I am everything but a fighter and I cannot shoot a gun if my life did depend on it”

Isadora snickered. “Me neither, I tried to shoot my dad’s old shotgun once and ended on my rear. I am glad those used to it can handle that part of it”

Brent smiled and gave her a swift hug. “I know you are worried about Thran but don’t be. Ty is good at what he is doing and they have drones and what not. It will be fine, the bastard will be caught”

Isadora just sighed. “Let us pray that you are right”

Thor was feeling very restless as the ranch prepared for the night, the workers had gone out and inn of the stables as usual even when there weren’t any animals in there, and the soldiers had recorded the daily sounds and were playing them, just to make it seem as if everything was normal. Frank was ready too, and obviously rather eager, his eyes were shining. “I hope we can fuck up that son of a bitch, he does deserve a nice old beating”

Thor had to grin, the younger man was ferocious. “I agree, but I would like to do more than beat him, let us just say it involves am electric cattle prod and certain bodily orifices”

Frank’s eyes got huge with delight. “Oh you have those here? Excellent, that would be a delight to see”

Thor sat down, it was dark around them and Frank patted his thigh. “I am carrying some heat, and two boxes of special mace. This gown is really neat, lots of places to hide stuff”

He pointed at the front of the gown and Thor had to laugh. “You hid the mace there?”

The young man nodded and looked like a rather upset damsel. “Of course Sir, and do keep your hands off, those things have sensitive…triggers”

Thor found that he did like this one, he managed to make the situation feel a lot less tense. Now they could only wait, and hope that things didn’t go to heck. The three men were an unknown factor after all, God alone knew what they were up to.

If they had been able to keep an eye on the ridge above the cattle pastures they would have been able to determine the whereabouts of at least one of the men Hemie had mentioned. It as Jake and he was crawling forwards, carrying two sticks of dynamite. The nice gentleman who had called him had promised that he would get even with that goddamn ranch owner, and that nobody would find out about his part in it.

It did sound like music in the ears of Jake, he hated the family and he hated everybody who failed to see what a spectacular genius he was. He ought to be running this place, not that overly tall pretty boy. Jake was incapable of keeping anything even resembling a job, he was simply too full of himself and he was completely unable to see that he was the problem. He thought the world owed him everything he wanted and when people did treat him like the piece of trash he was he usually lost it and became violent. His mother had spoiled him royally and allowed him to do everything he wanted to and she never tried to teach him any sorts of discipline. Jake was a narcissist and a psychopath and he wasn't able to realize that he was a loser in every possible manner.

Now he was given a golden chance to prove himself and the voice in the phone had been so filled with respect, even admiration. Now there was a person who truly saw Jake for what he was, worthy of everybody's respect, and worship. The idea of making the cattle stampede was the work of a genius, a mind similar to his own and he snickered as he sneaked forth along the ridge. He had gone to the place the voice said there would be stuff waiting for him and he had left the town so nobody could stop him. There were always some idiot cowboy watching the cows but they couldn't stop a real stampede, nobody could.

The dynamite was powerful and he felt that power like something physical, it almost made him physically aroused. He was gonna create mayhem, the idea was so very sweet and he grunted as he crawled forth between bushes and cacti. He had a lighter within his pants and he saw that the huge herd of cows was at rest. Stupid animals, but they were flighty and would level everything if they ran in the right direction. It was wonderful to think about. He was almost tempted to take a quick break and jerk off but decided against it, time for that afterwards. Jake was wearing his ordinary attire, worn out jeans, a shirt and a thin jacket, it was summer so it was rather warm, he didn't need much more and the colours were dim so it was hard to see him in the faint light of a crested moon. He hadn't visited the ranch in a long time, the last time he was there the old man had chased him off with several dogs and he didn't want a repetition of that again.

Jake stopped at the edge of the cliff and stared down, his small beady eyes were glittering. This was delightful, he would throw the dynamite behind those cows and then they would run, like never before. He took a look at his watch, the voice had mentioned a precise time but to heck with it, he didn't want to wait for yet another half an hour? What was the point in that? The cows would stampede and trample that goddamn ranch and it was all he cared about. He was about to reach into his pocket to retrieve the lighter when he heard something moving. He frowned. Was there somebody up there with him?

He listened. It did sound like an animal, not a human being. Bha, probably a coyote or some prairie dogs. Nothing to be afraid of. Jake was not a very tidy person, nor was he very cleanly. He hadn't changed his pants for weeks and his favourite dish or shall we say only dish was the local kebab, served at the fast food joint just outside of town. He ate there every day and grease and sauce had gathered in a thick layer on his pants, and it did smell. He was oblivious to that fact, but somebody else wasn't. There was a grunting sound and Jake turned his head again, what he saw made him squeal and get up.

It was a boar, a massive giant pig with huge tusks and eyes which glowed in the dark. This was the ghost of Hogzilla and Jake was perhaps an idiot but he knew that pigs are dangerous animals when they are feral. He tried to stay still, maybe that monster wouldn't bother him then. But Willy was hungry, and he felt a most alluring scent coming from that human. He hated humans, for they had hurt him many times, this one however didn't carry one of those dark sticks which made such sharp sounds and stung him. Willy raced forth, he was way faster than any human and he opened his jaw and grasped onto Jake's left thigh. The huge tusks sank deeply into the flesh but that side was where Jake also kept his lighter, and it got crushed in the attack. Jake screamed and he grasped a rock and hit the pig in the head with it.

The boar roared and reared back for a second and Jake stumbled backwards, the wound was pouring blood and he forgot about his whereabouts. He felt the ground give way underneath his feet and screamed again. Willy on the other hand loved the taste of the human blood and attacked again. The power of the impact finally knocked Jake over the edge of the cliff, and since Willy had grasped onto him again the pig too lost its footing and followed the screaming man over the edge. The fall was not that far, five meters, but it was enough. Jake hit the ground first and Willy followed and crushed the man completely.

The fall broke the pig's neck and the two bodies lay there, in a pile which started to produce smoke. The lighter in Jake's pocket was containing some very flammable fluids, they did react when exposed to oxygen and a small flame soon became a larger one. It was fed by clothing and soon both Willy and Jake was burning, a grease fire it would take a lot to put out. The cows didn't care, they were used to fires and this one didn't spread. The two had landed on clean rock, there was nothing there they could ignite. Some would perhaps say that there was a beautiful poetic justice at play there.

Thor and Frank was waiting in the living room, the house had lots of security installed and they felt safe but it was nerve wreaking not knowing what went on elsewhere. Thor was contemplating getting up to get a cup of tea when there was a crackling sound from one of the radios. "C2, this is C6, there is a small fire spotted up at the cattle pasture, over"

Frank grasped the radio. "This is C2, is it anything we should worry about?"

The voice at the other end did sound almost bored. "Nah, no danger. Probably an attempt at scaring the cattle"

Thor was about to let out a sigh of relief when they heard a very distinct boom through the radio, there was some silence and then the voice came back. "Holy fuck C2, there was an explosion"

Frank rolled his eyes. “Right C6, check it out, use the drone. Are the cows alright?”

The voice was gone for some seconds. “Yeah, they got startled but are already settling down again, sounded like dynamite though. But I will wait until daylight, my drone doesn’t have night vision and it is noisy, they may hear it if there are several people up there, I will stay alert though.”

Thor was blinking, his heart was racing. Dynamite? That was serious stuff for sure.

Frank did crinkle his nose and grinned. “Sounds like somebody tried to mess with your cows and got more than they bargained for”

Thor felt cold, his hands were shaking. Now it dawned upon him how serious this really was. “Let us hope that it is the only thing which happens tonight”

Frank pulled at his wig. “Wouldn’t bet on it. That sounded like a diversion to me”

Thor took a deep breath. “ One which didn’t work out the right way I would say”

The younger man tilted his head . “Exactly, so let us see what their next move is!”

The hidden stable had surveillance, there were cameras hidden around the entrance and Isadora and Brent had returned to their rooms and actually slept for a couple of hours when one of the workers discretely came to wake them up. Isadora rubbed her eyes and she felt rather terrible, the cot she had laid upon was hard and not at all comfortable. The worker had some mirth within her expression. “Get up folks, somebody is trying to get inn”

Brent was yawning and he rubbed his hair. “Really?”

The young lady nodded and smiled. “It is the Jonesby brothers, they know it is here you see, but they cannot get through the doors”

Brent and Isadora followed the girl to a small control room, the screens showed the area around the entrance and they saw a huge truck which was aiming its headlights at the area where the entrance was hidden. “Somebody showed them this when they were kids, they probably remember but they don’t know that the entrance has been reinforced since then. “

Brent frowned. “Why attack here? Do they know that Mr Oswold has hidden his horses here?”

The worker just shrugged. “There is a local belief that the old man used this site to hide a heck of a lot of wealth, a real treasure. We have had people trying to get into this place before, to no prevail. I bet those two dweebs think that they can get inside and fuck things up!”

Brent nodded slowly. “A perfect diversion right, I can see that. They probably know that there are bound to be alarms in here”

The girl giggled. “And that the treasure is just some hundred horses is something they are unaware of”

Isadora felt a bit odd, excited and also worried. “They cannot get through?”

The girl shook her head and rolled her eyes. “No, of course not. You could perhaps blast the doors open with a nuclear bomb but it can withstand anything less powerful than that.”

She pointed at the screen. “Look at those idiots?”

Isadora saw that they were trying to attach some dynamite to the artificial rock which made the camouflage. It didn’t exactly look elegant and they did take cover behind the huge truck. The blast which followed did nothing to the doors but a lot to the truck. Pebbles and gravel did rain and one of the brothers did pommel the other, probably because the truck had been too close and had damages to its paint job.

The girl snickered. “Everybody knows those two, the youngest one, Brian, is a bit retarded. We don’t know what diagnosis he has but his mom was drinking like a camel while she carried him so it isn’t hard to guess. And the oldest one, Tommy, is about as bright as a sheet of tar.”

Brent had to laugh. “The culprit knows how to pick his associates I see”

Isadora grunted. “He has picked people too dumb to understand that they are being used, that is the truth. Somebody able to hold a grudge without asking any questions as to why they suddenly have been given this opportunity. ¨

The worker shook her head in disbelief. “I have talked about this case with the others, they are all ready to defend the horses, with their lives if they have to. That bad guy sounds like somebody who ought to really taste some good old fashioned medicine"

Brent had an expression of slight curiosity upon his face. "I bet people around here has some ideas about what would be appropriate?"

The girl smiled, it did look sinister. "Oh we have, believe me we do. But it isn't for the squeamish to say the least. Many here are very peaceful people who wouldn't hurt a fly normally but this? It makes them reinvent the old manners of torture"

Isadora just shuddered. "I bet they do"

The images from outside showed that the larger brother was done beating the other one, then they got into the car and took off. The girl nodded at the guy controlling the cameras. "Tell base they are heading that direction"

The man nodded and sent a message and Brent did grasp Isadora's hand. "They will be waiting for them, do not worry"

Isadora tried to smile. She knew she shouldn't feel so nervous but she did. She would sit there and keep her fingers crossed.

The base in the ranch house was alerted of the two brothers, and they had moved the base from the stable into the kitchen. There was a cold locker there which was very large and also not a room people would visit unless they had to. It was perfect as a hideout and Thor had sent the chef and the kitchen workers home for the night. The two soldiers left there were busy with the cameras and the other equipment. Ty was by the old barn with Jason and the rest was spread around that area. All armed and all ready. The house was very quiet, and one soldier was placed on the cliff above the ranch, wearing night vision goggles. He was carrying a sniper rifle but was told only to shoot if the culprit did pose a threat to human lives. They had to be dead sure that this was the right person.

Everybody was waiting and Thor was feeling it as if his nerves were on the outside of his body, he was sweating. Frank sent him a stern glance. “Pull yourself together, this is important, stay calm”

Thor took a deep breath. “I am trying”

Frank took a look at his instruments and smiled. “I don’t think we have to wait for that much longer, if he is to strike tonight he has to do it soon”

Thor nodded. It was over two o clock and it was pitch darkness outside. “What about the two brothers?”

Frank just shrugged. “Do not worry, if we are out of here by the time they reach the place the others will take care of them”

Thor looked down. “I do not want anybody to be killed within my own home”

Frank scoffed. “Don’t worry man, not a drop of blood needs to be spilled, we are gonna leave a small present for them”

He did reach into a bag he had brought with him and produced two bottles of what seemed to be exquisite brand Whisky. Thor frowned. “Is that real?”

Frank nodded. “Yes, very good whisky, with a small list of added ingredients.”

He found some glasses and left them randomly around the table, then he poured some drops into them and made it look as if several people had been drinking there. One of the bottles was half full and he placed it on the table and left the other one on a shelf nearby. He rubbed his hands. “The brothers won’t be a problem, they will see the booze and go for it, and then they will say hello to the sandman for a while”

Frank went over and opened the door to the patio, left it slightly ajar. “Like that, they will be looking for a way inn and they won’t realize that they are being herded, like cattle.”

The small pad Frank was carrying started to beep and he ran over and lifted it. “Bingo, movement to the west of here. It is showtime”

Thor took a deep breath and closed his eyes. Now he could only hope that this didn’t end in disaster, one way or the other.

The soldier placed on the cliff had seen the man with his night vision goggles, they detected heat and the soldier turned on his camera and followed the faint dot of red light carefully. It was one person, moving slowly forth and he was carrying something, it did look cold and it was oblong. The soldier had some other goggles too, and he used them to confirm his suspicion. The culprit did carry a rocket launcher and what had to be several rockets on his back. The man had to have contacts. “C7 to C1, object in sight, carrying an RPG, over”

Three clicks was the answer, it told him that it was confirmed. The soldier made a grimace. He could have taken that man out there and then but Ty wanted him alive, too bad. He had a calibre 50 bullet there who would just love to kiss that bastard goodnight. He just kept watching as the man walked forth along one of the animal tracks, silently and with obvious determination.

The man who was making his way along the path was panting, if there had been daylight one could have seen that his face was blood red but it wasn’t from the fact that he was carrying some pretty heavy equipment over difficult terrain. No, it was because he was angry, shaking with wrath. His plans had been thwarted, by some goddamn terrorist. He had been ready for that competition, he had even managed to get his hands on several bombs from an abandoned army storage facility. With a plane he could have levelled everything to the ground. It would have been perfect. But he would have to wait. Just because some scarf wearing religious nutcase didn’t see eye to eye with some of the drivers. It shouldn’t be his problem.

He had found that article though, and it was such a relief to see that his mission wouldn’t be forced to lay dormant for very long. He would take his revenge, on the goddamn beasts which dared to steal what had been his, what should have been his all along. He hated them, hated seeing them in the news, being bragged about, it should have been him, his fame, his place in the sun, in the limelight.

The ranch was large and he was looking forward to blowing those stables sky high, it was what they all deserved. There had to be some surveillance but he had been smart, the town was small but there are bad apples in every crate and that cretin at the sheriff's office had been more than willing to chat with him. The man named Jake was so easy to manipulate it wasn't even fun and the brothers were dimwits too. People here in these parts of the country probably married their twelve year old cousins rather often, inbreeding was helpful when it came to creating useful twats. He wouldn't help them afterwards, no, he would leave the whole mess on them, it was really very neat.

He would have loved to bomb the place from above but he cursed the fact that the rules did require for a plane to have a beacon these days, he didn't want to be shot down by some suspicious jet fighter pilot. The crop duster had been easy enough to get his hands on, the pilot was a drunk and some poison in the whiskey had sent him to the other side fast, then it was easy to prepare the plane and the fluids, he had torched the plane afterwards. He had flown underneath the radar and blessed the fact that he had taken flying lessons as a kid, not they were put to good use. Nobody could find him, he was superior to them all, a star, a winner. He was the one everybody should have worshipped.

The drive over there had been long and not very comfortable but he had made it and the last day he had been laying in hiding in his mobile home at a road side café. He had pretended to have a flat wheel and people seemed to swallow that lie. To call those three had been easy and not they were out there, somewhere.

He got closer to the ranch, the place did seem quiet, and normal. He had seen some satellite photos of the place and knew where he was and he was almost shaking with eager anticipation when he started to prepare the rocket launcher. The buildings did seem sturdy though, but they would burn, he was sure they would burn. A couple of rockets would probably do the job rather well.

He had found an excellent spot to shot from and he cursed the darkness. The area around the stable was dark, he wasn't able to see anything except the shape of the first building and some faint light from within it. But you cannot miss such a huge target. He waited however, the man he had hired ought to have spooked those cows rather well by now, it was five minutes since he ought to have set off that dynamite.

He waited, the herd would use some time to run that far but cattle are fast when they do stampede and the chaos would be sure to hide his whereabouts. Five minutes went by, ten, fifteen. Not a sound, not a moo. He cursed to himself, the jackass had probably screwed things up, he should have anticipated that. Jake was a drunkard after all and if he had a watch that was correct it would be a miracle. Right, he couldn't wait anymore, it would get harder to get away of it the sun started to rise again and to heck with that goddamn idiot.

The cowboys could catch him and fry him for all he cared, but he was rather sure that the brothers would create at least some distraction, they did seem capable of almost anything. Real good old fashioned rednecks, too stupid to ask any questions and very fond of explosions. He got the launcher up onto his shoulder and aimed, his heart beating and sweat flowing off him. They would repay for what they had done to him.

He fired and the rocket did scream into the night and was gone and he waited for the flash and the boom but nothing happened. He frowned, was it a blank? It had to be. He found another one and prepared it, he was starting to feel a bit nervous. He didn't see the black drone which hovered above the area and the device it carried, made to deactivate any sorts of electronic devices, like the fuse of a rocket.

The next rocket flew and it did hit something with a bang, the wall did burst into flame but the explosion wasn't as grand as he had anticipated, he hadn't tried to fire a rocket at a solid timber wall and didn't know that the walls were reinforced due to the danger of flash floods and huge amounts of snow in winter. That rocket had been flying too fast to be caught by the signals from the drone, the soldier operating it hadn't had time to aim the device.

He growled to himself but he realized that something was missing, there was no whinnying, no sounds of horses at all. Were all the goddamn nags out there on the pastures? Heck, he hadn't gone through all this to be disappointed. There were no horses near the ranch, he had seen that so where were they?

He did see that somebody did leave the building which had to be the main house of the ranch, he had seen that tall blonde before, the owner wasn't he? A very talented rider. And that brunette following him was also a rider, well, if they were off to check on the horses he would not let this opportunity pass him by. He laid the launcher down, it was too heavy to carry for long but he had a gun and he felt that the hatred he felt gave him extra strength. He had planned on poisoning the entire herd there using a drone and some nasty germs he had acquired over the net but he had wanted to really enjoy this in person too. Hearing the screams of horses was what kept him going. They would scream as he had screamed. He did rub the false underarm, it did still hurt even if it wasn't really there anymore.

He ran after the two who drove off on a small ATV, slowly as they obviously were chatting to each other. The woman was leaning close to the man and holding onto him and they followed a road which did lead away from the ranch. Perfect! He was no long distance runner but he could keep up, the darkness made it easy to keep an eye on the red backlights from the vehicle.

Frank was hiding his screen behind Thor's back, he whispered. "We have movements, behind us. He is taking the bait. Keep going, slowly"

Thor was panting. "The fire?!"

Frank whispered back. "Don't worry, the workers will put it out the moment we are far enough away from the ranch buildings. The log walls do not burn very well and the rocket didn't do much damage, the drone did prevent the head of it from exploding, it was just the fuel which caught fire"

Thor nodded, he felt oddly disconnected, the culprit was behind them somewhere, following them. He remembered what that man had done to his horse and many others and something akin to anger did awaken within him and not the red hot blazing type he was used to. No, this was cold, freezing cold. He did keep a slow pace, pretended to stop to admire the stars every now and then and Frank did play his role rather well, he was careful not to show his face for if the culprit had night vision goggles he could possibly see that the profile was wrong. He did however play the role of a damsel rather well and used a feminine body language.

They were approaching the old barn, Ty and Jason and also a couple of the other soldiers were there somewhere, well hidden and Thor felt that his heart was racing. He stopped the ATV and the two of them walked forth, arm in arm. Frank bowed down a bit, he was too tall to be mistaken for a woman but it helped that Thor was such an extremely tall man. Now they could only hope that the bastard took the bait and exposed himself, Ty was ready and Thor was very glad he had a vest on.

Ty was laying in wait, they were all using very good equipment but even those good inventions couldn't have foreseen what would happen next. The man had carried more than just an RPG, he had something in his belt and Ty saw that the man who came in from behind the bushes tossed it towards the two out there. He was about to cry out to warn them but it was too late. An intense light and a strong bang was heard, it was a flashbang grenade and it left them all blinded for a few seconds. The night vision goggles made every man there blink and wipe their eyes, they were unable to see anything.

Thor felt a powerful thrust to his upper body and fell, it made him see white light and he realized that the man had shot him. He knew what to do, he remained laying down. Frank was spinning around but the culprit was already there, grasping onto the brunette with one arm, knocking him over the head with the other one. Frank was a trained soldier, he also knew how to make things hard for a kidnapper. He pretended to pass out, and with 175 pounds he wasn't a dainty flower. The man was grunting as he dragged the seemingly unconscious "woman" towards the barn.

He would interrogate her there, find out where all the nags where, then he would shoot them all. He was surprised by the weight of the woman and bent down to get a better grip of her, just as Ty fired off his odd looking rifle. The small dart hit the man straight on the arse instead of in the back and the man screamed and let go of the woman, the dart had contained a mixture of several drugs which normally would bring anybody to their knees in a matter of seconds but the man was a wee bit on the fluffy side and his ass had so much fat only a little of the drugs hit his system. It just hurt like hell and he swore like a sailor and grasped his gun again, fine, if that was how they played he would just shot that fucking whore and walk off, finding the horses on his own. He was so full of adrenaline he didn't even think about the fact that the dart had to come from somewhere.

Jason was trembling with supressed energy and Ty was swearing and rubbing his eyes. "Fuck, I missed."

He grasped the radio. "Do take him out, do it now, he'll shoot Frank!"

The soldiers placed on the other side of the pasture weren't that affected by the grenade and one of them did obey immediately. He did take aim and did what he was taught to do to bring something down, he shot at the legs. One bullet came buzzing and the man screamed as he was hit through the calf of his right leg. The injury should really be enough but this was not an ordinary person anymore, he was driven by adrenaline and sheer pure anger and hatred.

It had been a trap, he was gonna make them pay. His system started to react to the drugs now, his vision was swimming and he roared with rage, grasped onto the female again and dragged her after him, towards the barn. He could make his stand in there, with the woman alive he could use her as a hostage. Yes, that was the way. He would make them parade all those goddamn horses out in front of the barn one by one so he could shoot them all, if not he would cut that bitch up, slowly. He had several knives and he wasn't afraid to be rough. She deserved it, for being one who did care for those beasts.

Frank was dizzy and he wasn't sure of what to do, he had to pretend to be unconscious, even he couldn't dodge a bullet from such a short distance and he could only hope that he would get the chance to get the mace from the stuffed bra. The man was hissing and groaning and the sounds did resemble those of a mad animal, he dragged Frank into the darkness of the barn and stopped when it was completely dark. He was grinning, a wild wide grin, oh yes, he would slice that bitch into thin strips and then he would throw them out there, one by one. He was so overwhelmed by adrenaline, hatred and anger he failed to realize that they weren't alone in the barn. The darkness did hide the one being who used to stay within this barn and he was impossible to spot. But Frank felt him, felt the energy of the massive beast and a faint streak of moonlight came inn through a tiny crack.

Outside Thor quickly crawled into cover behind a stone, he was suddenly aware of the smell of horse and his eyes got huge, he couldn't allow that this beast hurt Petite. He took a deep breath and put all his hope into one desperate move. He grasped a stone and threw it into the barn. Frank had seen that Thor got up and grasped the stone and he let out a thin wail as if he was a woman waking up and Thor threw towards the sound.

The man was feeling faint, everything was glassy and he saw that the man out there had gotten up and that he did throw something towards him. His instincts told him to get away from it, it could be a weapon, a grenade or something. So he took some steps backwards, keeping an eye on the man out there if he started to get closer.

The sudden feeling of hot breath against his scalp was not one he anticipated, neither was the feeling of colliding with something massive. He felt the scent and a bout of panic grasped him. he was grasping for his gun but it was too late. Pete had seen how Thor had fallen, and he could smell that this human was no good, he smelled of something nasty, something which made the huge horse lay his ears back. Pete was the gentlest and most caring soul out there, with a heart the size of a country. But he was a stallion, and his job was to protect his band. Thor was a part of his band, and this man, this stranger, was an intruder. He didn't accept that strangers hurt his friends, his humans.

A massive head with jaws powerful enough to tear a limb apart descended upon the man's left arm underneath the shoulder, grasped it and crushed it between long yellow teeth before lifting the man off the ground. To a giant like Petite it was no problem, not even a challenge. The human was like a mosquito to him.

The man screamed and tried to hit the horse with the prosthetic arm, that only made Petite shake his head and the man had already dropped the gun, the arm wasn't functioning anymore. He didn't have true grip within his right hand, the prosthetic arm wasn't that modern, he was howling with pain and anger and the horror of what was happening was getting control of him. He tried to grasp a knife with the right hand, to stab the monster which held him but he couldn't twist around and Petite let out a loud sound, the battle scream of a stallion, it did pierce the night and reminded everybody of a loud siren. If the man had used his brain he would have stopped struggling, but he wasn't sane, he was crazy.

He kept struggling and Pete did what he had to do. He threw the man down, then he reared up and let his entire weight of more than a ton of muscle and bone land on the man's legs and lower body. The bones broke like toothpicks and the man passed out from the pain, they could hear the sounds, as if from cracking timbers. Frank backed away from the snorting giant, and Thorran into the barn, Ty and Jason was right behind him, carrying flashlights.

They stopped, Pete was dancing, massive hooves almost the size of manhole covers thundered against the ground and the scent of blood made the horse roll his eyes and snort. Thor raised his arms. "It is me Pete, just me. Easy old boy, easy. It is over, the danger is over"

Ty bent down over the man, he was a bit pale. He hadn't anticipated the flash bang and he turned the flashlight towards the fallen enemy. "Now, let us see who this prick is"

Thor calmed the horse down, he listened to Thor and since this well known human was calm he relaxed too, the nostrils stopped flaring and the eyes got less wild. Frank rubbed his head. "Do you see who it is?"

Ty did shake his head, "I don't know, he is badly hurt though. Should we call for an air ambulance?"

Jason was panting, he had been running. "I have seen him before, I just don't know where or when. But it must have been some years ago"

Thor stared at the wounded man, the face was contorted by a terrible mixture of anger and hatred and it was justice there, a murderer of horses, murdered by a horse. "Know what? We didn't see this, this guy brought it onto himself. We just found him"

Ty was smiling, the grin a very nasty one. "Right, some animal found him first yeah?"

Thor nodded. "We have bears here, and coyotes. I don't want people to know that Pete here killed a guy"

Ty smiled widely. "Of course not, such a noble animal."

He grasped the radio. "C1 here, the culprit is dead…he got mauled by a….bear"

Jason swallowed. "He is alive?"

Ty just spat. "Not for long, he is bleeding out fast. Would be too late even with the air ambulance. No, the world is better off without this piece of shit"

The other soldiers looked as if they wanted to kick the dying man. "The filth ought to burn, but that will look suspicious"

Frank grasped the man by a foot and dragged him out of the barn, in the moonlight he was a terrible sight. The soldier did rummage through the pockets and found a wallet, he did open it and found a card. "Guys, say hello and farewell to Mr Dennis Cropsfield"

Jason snapped his fingers. "Right, I have that name somewhere and also the face, now I made the connection"

He pointed at the body laying at their feet. "He was an actor, about twenty years ago"

Ty frowned. “Oh yeah, I remember, he had several good movies too. He was a rising star for sure”

Thor tilted his head and stared at the bloody face. “Darn it, I recognize him now that you mention it. But he disappeared?”

Jason nodded, he was almost shaking with excitement. “Yes, yes, there was an accident during the preparations for a movie. He lost an arm and got a lot of scars.”

Jason did kneel down and wiped some of the blood of the face, the man was grey and wheezing, he was dying fast. “See?”

They saw that there were rather nasty scars all over the face, they had contorted the features and transformed a very handsome person into somebody who did look slightly deformed. Ty raised a finger to his chin. “But what does that have to do with horses, he obviously wanted to kill each and every one of them?”

Jason smiled, relieved beyond belief and oddly satisfied with the outcome. “The accident was caused by a horse, during the filming. The animal spooked and backed into some equipment which fell over Mr Cropsfield, maiming him pretty badly. I am an idiot, I should have thought of that incident. The rumours said that Mr Cropsfield shot that horse afterwards, out of sheer spite. But he disappeared and I had forgotten all about him”

There was a wheezing sound and the former actor stopped breathing. “Did he have family?”

Jason shrugged. “I can find out. Leave the body here for now, tomorrow the local wildlife will have covered the cause of death for sure”

Thor smiled slowly, there was an odd light in his eyes. “There are some wolves in this valley, they will come as soon as we disappear. The scent of blood will draw them inn”

Ty gathered his things. “Good, let’s go. I am dying of thirst here”

Jason did snicker. “A stiff drink would be nice yes. And Thor?!”

The tall blonde did nod. “Yes?”

Jason pointed towards the huge black horse. “Give old Pete some extra love ha? Some extra oats or something?”

Thor smiled. “He’ll get a sack of carrots first thing in the morning”

Frank stared at the massive horse. “The predators aren’t a danger to him I hope?”

Thor did snort. “I would like to see the wolf or bear which dares to make a move towards Pete, he will crush them to a pulp, nah, they stay clear of him, all of them do. They know death when they see it”

Pete did snort, as if to say end of discussion.

Back at the ranch the two brothers had reached the main buildings, there weren’t anybody there at all and that was odd but the two men grinned widely to each other. This was going the right way after all, they could trash the place unhindered. The patio doors were ajar and they were sneaking inside, the living room was large and very luxurious but their eyes fell on the bottles on the table. It was very fine whisky, way better than the swill they usually drank and they didn't let this chance pass them by. They grasped a glass each and poured themselves some stiff drinks with a lack of elegance which would have made any bar keeper swoon with shock. The whiskey was excellent, just as smooth and tasty as they had anticipated. Darn, these rich people, they really had it made hadn't they? One glass wasn't enough, they just grasped the bottles and chugged down straight from it, not very elegant and whiskey was running down their chins. They burped and sat down, eyes swimming and out of focus and with a feeling of euphoria both did fall asleep. With the drugs in the whiskey it would take the trumpets of the day of judgement to wake them up.

They were still sleeping when Thor and the others arrived, they had notified Isadora and Brent that the danger was over and Jason was on the phone, trying to get more information about the now dead culprit. Ty stared at the two men, they were stinking and both were rather obese and they couldn't know what water was for at all. "Should I make them disappear?"

Thor did hesitate. "Well, it is tempting and thanks for the offer but no, we cannot have too many deaths here just in one night. No, let them live but know what? Make sure they learn a lesson"

Ty smiled, a very slow smile which wasn't at all pretty, it showed that his man could be cruel. "That is understood boss, Frank, get the guys to prepare these two prime specimen for a Russian wedding"

Thor frowned. “A Russian wedding?”

It looked as if he didn’t truly want to know what that was but Ty snickered. “You will find out, eventually”

Two of the other soldiers came and the brothers were hauled outside and disappeared into the night, Thor had a feeling that they would regret accepting that job, for the rest of their lives.

Isadora and Brent came driving from the stable, Isadora threw herself at Thor who embraced her just as vigorously but flinched as she grasped onto him. “Oh my god, are you hurt?”

He did pat the vest. “No, just a wee bit tender, thanks to this”

Isadora almost sobbed. “Oh thank God you wore it”

Ty nodded and smiled. “I would never have allowed him to not wear one.”

Brent stared at the empty whisky bottles and he was squinting, “Do I want to know?”

Thor made a sheepish grin. “Probably not”

Isadora was still breathing a bit fast, she had been so terribly worried. “And the culprit is dead, for sure? You are absolutely certain?”

Thor took a deep breath. “Yes, absolutely certain. 110% certain, he is flat, shot, drugged. The body will be recovered tomorrow, whatever is left of it that is!”

Isadora closed her eyes. “So it was an actor…”

Jason nodded, he put down the phone. “Yes, I have checked his information now. He was very popular and also a very arrogant person before the accident, he was assumed to be of those who can just fill their shelves with Oscars. But the accident made him snap"

Brent sat down, he looked tired. "But that is no excuse now is it?"

Jason sighed. "He did try to fix it, went to therapy. Then his wife left him for a horse trainer and well, the final drop and all. The therapist disappeared, was found dead some weeks later. He had been bludgeoned to death with a hammer. Nobody suspected that Mr Cropsfield was behind it but it was probably him."

He did hold up the phone, there was some text on it. "Says here that he did work as a salesman, for an agricultural firm which sells fencing poles among other things. He managed to lay low, his mental state probably deteriorated gradually"

Thor nodded. "Like removing a wee bit at a time from a dam, sooner or later it does collapse"

Jason made a grimace. "I am rather sure that he hated horses both for being the cause of his lost career and for getting the attention he no longer got. He was stark raving mad"

Brent nodded. "Amen to that"

Outside the sun was starting to rise, there was some smoke but the fire had been put up and the rocket hadn't really done that much damage to the stable. A few logs would have to be replaced but otherwise from that they didn't need to do much. Jason was on the phone again with the sheriff and it was a sort of understanding between them regarding the brothers and Jake. They had no idea of where that man was but they would find out. Ty had asked the man he had stationed out there to check out the explosion as soon as it got light, as he had suggested he would. It was probably Jake who was behind it. The cows were calm so he hadn't had much luck if his goal was to create a stampede.

The workers started to return, many were almost in tears due to relief and they hugged Thor and there was a festive mood there. Thor did get some bottles of wine and opened them and there was cheering for sure. The soldiers came back from their positions and Ty received a call from the man by the cow pastures. He had checked out the explosion all right and found the scorched remains of a man and a huge hog, embraced in death. It did look like the barbeque from hell as he said, and smelled like one too and Thor sat down and laughed for a very long time.

It seemed that Willy the boar had gotten a Viking burial, complete with a slave to follow him into the afterlife and all and if fate was kind the huge boar would be greeted in the great halls as a hero for he had most certainly thwarted a very nasty part of Mr Cropsfield's plans. And the area had gotten rid of a nasty problem too.

The body of Mr Cropsfield was retrieved by a couple of the workers who dealt with dead animals, it wasn't that much left of it though. The huge horse who used to stay by the barn at night had stepped on the body again, just a few times, as if to make sure that the nasty human was no more. He was flatter than a dance floor as one of the guys put it. And the wolves had been there too and eaten what wasn't flattened. So you could gather what was left of the man in a bucket. Jason promised to get everything organized, the official cause of death would be animal attack, not even the best coroner could dispute that now. Mr Cropsfield did only have one living relative, an aunt who was living at a retirement home and she was so senile she probably didn't even know she had a nephew. So the urn would be sent to her but it would probably just be interred at the local churchyard without much more ado.

Isadora was so relieved it was over she was crying and then she cried for Adagio and the others who had died and she and Thor slept close to each other that day. She felt like she woke up from a bad dream when she finally was retrieved from the land of dreams by Thor. He had delightful news for her. He had found out what a Russian wedding was, the two brothers had been taken out into the wilderness, stripped and dressed in a ballet gown and a pair of arseless leather pants. They had been chained to each other with handcuffs, ankle to ankle and wrist to wrist and they hadn't anything on their feet.

When they made it back to the town they were hardly able to move, sunburned and thirsty and almost eaten alive by gnats. Frank had added to their torment by smearing them with a substance which attracted insects. The two had to flee the town, their reputation was ruined, it is no point in trying to be a bully when everybody has seen you like that, people would just laugh at them now.

Jason left and Brent too had to return to Crested Moon, he did hug them all goodbye and promised to let them know when he found out what would happen regarding the mare. Isadora was somewhat glad that she and Thor was left alone, the ranch had returned to the normal daily routine and things had eased down. She was still uncertain about her professional future, she had no horse and she didn't have enough money to buy a good one right now. Her butt was still rather sore and she did curse that fact again and again, she wanted to take Thor to bed and stay there but he refused to go that far until she was fully healed, as he said it, she would need her strength if she was to bed him. She was unsure if that was said in jest or if he meant it. A part of her hoped for the last alternative for darn, she felt like a bitch in heat whenever he was near her.

Then one morning she got up and he was gone, a note was left on the nightstand. "Get dressed and meet me by the stable, wear riding gear"

She felt a bit uncertain but did as she had been told. She had to gasp as she approached the now fixed stable, Thor stood there with two horses, one was the large dark grey horse named General Flint and the other the oddly coloured mix breed she had admired before. Starfall was saddled and did look like a fairytale horse, the large eyes were shining and he was pawing the ground. Thor did grin. "My workers said you liked him so why not try him out? He needs some exercise."

Isadora swallowed. "I…he is magnificent, but…you think I can handle him?"

Thor winked. "I have told him to behave, come on"

She forced back the feeling of insecurity and got in the saddle, the horse was taller than Adagio had been and more long legged and also, he felt like a volcano. An immense amount of power, barely reined inn. Thor got up on General Flint and smiled. “Follow me”

He rode off towards an area Isadora hadn’t seen before and she was stunned to find several huge training areas for different disciplines, both show jumping and cross country riding. Thor let General Flint go over into a gallop and rode towards the first jumps and Starfall snapped at the bitt and wanted to go. She took a deep breath and let the horse have free reins, he took off like a rocket and she had a feeling of just being a passenger there and then. But the stallion surprised her, he listened to her and he approached the hurdles like an experienced horse, one with years of competitions behind him and when they did finish the track she knew she never had ridden a better horse. Adagio hadn’t had this explosive extra gear, which made him able to more or less fly over the hurdles and cover ground like a cheetah.

She was enthralled and Thor grinned widely as they stopped. The huge grey horse had been awesome too, but he was slower and took the hurdles differently. It was obvious that he preferred to plan ahead and was more careful. Starfall just went for it, with no fear and hesitation and Isadora loved it, it was just the way she liked it.

The tall blonde did tilt his head. “Now, did you like him?”

Isadora nodded. “Yes, oh yes, he is…perfect”

She felt jealous, Thor owned a true star there, a horse which would enthral the public. He reached over and took her hand. "Good, he is yours"

Isadora had to gasp and she couldn't believe what she had heard. "Are you kidding me? He is worth…"

Thor just snickered. "A lot, yes, but you are worth more to me. And it is normal for a man to buy his future wife gifts"

She blinked. "Ah…Uh…are you proposing to me?"

She couldn't believe it but he got off the general and kneeled down. Isadora had to get off Starfall too and he pulled out a ring. It wasn't a diamond, it was a fire opal, red and absolutely spectacular. "Yes, would you do me the tremendous honour of becoming my wife?"

Isadora fell to her knees. "Yes, yes you big…oaf, yes!"

He embraced her and kissed her with an impressive amount of passion. "You just made me a very happy man, and believe me, tonight I will make you a very happy woman. I went to town this morning, I have a new pack of condoms"

She had to laugh, and she kept laughing as he got her back onto her feet. Starfall grasped a lock of her hair and started chewing on it and they both stood there, shaking with mirth.

That evening the housekeeper was told to leave early and she snickered as she cleared away the plates from dinner, the tension within the house was very obvious. She was rather sure that happy news would be shared rather soon.

The next morning Isadora and Thor barely showed their faces at all until rather late and Isadora had a funny gait and looked like a cat which has found a very large bowl of cream and Thor was very cheerful indeed. The workers joked that they ought to go and ask for a raise for he probably would agree to just about anything this morning.

Isadora had realized that he hadn't been jesting at all, and he was more than capable of making her squirm and scream and that pack of condoms had to be replaced by a new one rather fast.

A week later they received a call from Brent over skype, he was in an odd mood, both angry and amused at the same time. Mr Berners granddaughter had indeed decided that her daughter ought to get the benefit of riding a very experienced horse and had cancelled the contract with Brent, even if Mr Berner's will had been very clear. Brent was to have Crested Moon, the mare was his, period. He had tried to protest but the granddaughter had lawyers and they were good, claiming that Mr Berner had been suffering from early stage dementia when he wrote his will.

Brent sent them the movie file, of the great granddaughter showing up at a contest, with Crested Moon. Isadora didn't like the girl at all, the file was very good and showed that this was one royally spoiled kid who probably never had been allowed to fail at anything. The mare looked good as always, Brent said that Mr Berner's granddaughter had gotten a very good groom for her and she was cared for in an excellent manner. But it was obvious that the mare didn't like Patricia at all. Isadora held her breath, she was waiting for it. This wasn't a top level competition at all, it was more or less the local pony club and a mare like Crested Moon didn't fit in at that level, it was an insult to her.

The horse was obviously annoyed with the noise and the general chaos there and Patricia used a mounting block to get up. She couldn't have tried the mare at all and Thor snickered. "She looks like a sack of oats, she needs to shed at least two stones."

Isadora held her breath, this could end badly but Brent had sounded almost triumphant. Patricia gave the mare of her heels and Crested Moon freaked out, she rushed forth and started to buck. Brent could be heard over the phone. "She has ticklish flanks, you cannot use your legs that way with her"

Patricia managed to hang on for a few moments, then she flew. And she flew far, in an elongated curve which lead straight to the nearest manure heap. The girl landed face first, in steaming horse shit and the spotless riding attire wasn't that spotless anymore. She got up, screaming and bawling and several of the spectators were gathering, whispering and laughing. "I hate her, I hate her, get rid of her"

The girl was screaming from the top of her lungs and Crested Moon stood there and looked smug, the mare was grinning, Isadora could have sworn it. Patricia's mother looked as if she was about to have a heart attack, her eyes were bulging. One of the other riders came over, a very distinguished elderly gentleman. "What is that mare doing here? She belongs to Mr Brewster, everybody in the club heard that Mr Berner was to sign her over to Brent. You don't really believe that your little spoiled lump of grease can ride a horse like that?"

The woman was gaping and others there stood there, booing. "Hear, hear!"

Many of the parents had been angry since Patricia had gotten such a good horse compared with their own kids and it wasn't fair but Patricia's mom probably knew the judges and had found a way to twist her way through the rules. Now they couldn't ignore it anymore, too many had seen that Patricia were unable to handle such a large and high strung animal, "Send the mare to her rightful owner, who knows how to ride such an exquisite animal"

Patricia was bawling. "I want another horse, I want a kind one."

The elderly chap smiled, it was a foul smile. "Listen to your daughter, get her a rocking horse, she cannot handle anything more frisky poor thing"

Brent did end the movie file, he was snickering. "Two hours later Crested Moon was mine, papers signed and all. She is in my stable again, where she belongs"

He did wink at them. "I have heard that a congratulation is in order, and you are both to return to the competitions?"

Thor nodded. "I must confess that yes, there is a wedding coming up soon. And yes, we will both compete again, we both have good new horses"

Brent looked at Isadora. "That golden black of yours will turn heads, believe me. And General Flint is majestic, people will love him. I am looking forwards to competing against you both, finally a real challenge again. "

Thor snickered. "Yeah, but the general is not a good dressage horse and Starfall is a bit hot headed still, you have good chances now. But sooner or later…!"

Brent laughed. "We'll see"

Isadora did wave at him. "You are welcome to the wedding, you must promise me to come, bring Joel!"

Brent nodded and smiled at them. "I promise"

He did end the call with a wink.

Thor turned to Isadora. "I have a small idea"

She grinned. "Small? Noting about you is small…"

He snickered and kissed the tip of her nose. "We are happy and I think Brent does deserve that happiness too. He and Joel ought to be able to show the world that they love each other don't you think?"

Isadora raised an eyebrow. "Ah, I wonder what that expression upon your face mean? Oh I know, you are gonna be devious again aren't you?"

He grinned and lifted her up. "Indeed I am"

Two weeks later they did celebrate a rather grand wedding at the local church. Somebody had suggested that the bride and groom ought to be driven to and fro the church by horse and carriage and Isadora had agreed. But she hadn't had any idea of what horse the workers would use. Somebody had gotten Petite and brushed and groomed him, the hooves were oiled, the feathers neatly trimmed and the harness was special made with lots of brass and silver and the giant did look amazing. The black fur was shining like oil and the long mane and tail were braided and decorated with white ribbons. The wagon was also a rare and very valuable relic of the past and it had belonged to Thor's grandfather. It revealed that there was some rather blue blood somewhere in the family tree for it had a very obvious crest on the side.

Isadora was perfectly happy and the ceremony and the party afterwards was perfection. Thor was beaming and they had gotten a lot of very nice presents.

Linda was there too, she had returned to Isadora and now she was in charge of Isadora's own farm Springwell, a huge jump upwards when it came to career but one she was more than capable of doing. Being a ranch administrator was probably a better solution for her than being a rider due to her busted knee. Many of the other riders they knew were there also and Brent and Joel was having a very good time. Nobody there cared if they showed that they were partners. Thor was waiting for the right moment and it came, he sauntered over to the two and Brent greeted him, holding Joel by the hand. "Goddamn it Thor, it makes me want to get married too"

Thor just shrugged. "Then why don't you?"

Brent sighed. "You know how it is? My aunt. If she finds out I will lose everything, I will have to start again from scratch"

Thor did tilt his head, a devil was dancing within those blue eyes. “Are you sure?”

Brent frowned. “Ah, what are you up to….don’t tell me that…”

Thor did pull some papers out from inside his jacket. “Here, it is a gift”

Jason had been invited too and he stood there, wide eyed. “Holy shit man, don’t tell me that you did buy the whole business?!”

Brent opened the papers and let out a squeal, tears filled his eyes and Joel did gasp, he was staring at Thran as if he had seen a ghost. “Thor…I…”

Thor did just grin, casually. “You know, your aunt is not very smart, she was the sole owner of all those factories and she has run them the same way they have been run for over fifty years. You are bound to lose money like that.”

Brent was just panting. “But she is out of the equation now, I bought her out. And there are new people employed there, who will make the business earn money again. The coffers were close to empty Brent, you would have lost everything anyhow. But now you are the owner and can do what you want with the whole thing”

Brent was crying and Joel sobbed and everybody was clapping and cheering. Isadora had to dry off some tears too. She knew that Thor was among the most wealthy people she had ever met and he was more than capable of sharing his wealth.

Soon they would return to the competitions and she was glad that her husband never would allow her to win just to please her, it would be a challenge just like before and she squealed as he lifted her off the floor and kissed her. “I feel like retiring for the night Mrs Oswold, what about you?”

She kissed him back and the crowd was cheering like mad. “I agree Mr Oswold, I do agree fully!”

He spun around and carried her through the door, the ranch had been decorated to welcome them home and Pete was standing there, obediently chewing on his bit. Isadora did pet him an extra time. Thanks to Pete they got to experience this and she was very grateful indeed. Thor grasped the reins. “Let’s go?”

She nodded. “Indeed, let’s face the future. Giddyup Petite”

The stallion nickered and trotted off and Isadora leaned against the wide shoulder next to her and knew that the future did look grand, better than it ever had been. Yes, she was blessed, and even though the memories of the horrors never would fully fade the tragedies had brought something good too. She had a wonderful husband and a wonderful horse and Brent and Joel would probably tie the knot soon too. There was much to rejoice and so she did, wholeheartedly and with gratitude.

The end.

www.ingramcontent.com/pod-product-compliance
Lightning Source LLC
LaVergne TN
LVHW012055160826
845678LV00014B/2834

* 9 7 8 8 2 9 3 3 5 5 5 9 5 *